ALSO BY KIMBERLY MULLINS:

Notebook Mysteries ~ Emma (Book 1)

Notebook Mysteries ~ Decisions and Possibilities (Book 2)

Notebook Mysteries ~ Changes and Challenges (Book 3)

Notebook Mysteries ~ Unexpected Outcomes (Book 4)

Notebook Mysteries ~ Haunted Christmas (a novella)

Notebook Mysteries ~ Suspicions (Book 5)

Notebook Mysteries ~ Parisian Intrigue (Book 6)

Notebook Mysteries ~ A Party to Remember (a novella)

Notebook Mysteries ~ Art of Deception (Book 7)

Notebook Mysteries ~ The Twelve Days of Murder (a novella)

Stand alones:

Divided Lives (K.R. Mullins)

1897-A Mark Sutherland Adventure

Lights, Camera, Murder!!!

The Family Business

Notebook Mysteries

Notebook Mysteries

Murderous
Christmas
Mischief

KIMBERLY
MULLINS

NOTEBOOK MYSTERIES ~ MURDEROUS CHRISTMAS MISCHIEF

Notebook Mysteries Series

Copyright © JKJ books, LLC 2025

First edition: December 2025

Contact: kimberlymullinsauthor.com

Library of Congress Control Number:

ISBN (paperback): 989-8-9938502-0-7

ISBN (hardback): 979-8-9938502-1-4

ISBN (ebook): 979-8-991-6865-9-4

This is a work of fiction. It is based on historical events within Chicago during the time period of the 1880-90's.

Edited by Kaitlyn Johnson, Strictly Textual

Cover Art by Miblart

Christmas is a wonderful time, we love the eggnog, the lights, the movies. Special thanks to Jonathan for the idea for this novella. The my best boy, Joshua, I can't wait until Christmas morning. To Claudia, the first person I want to read my books.

CHAPTER 1

The fog clouded her vision as Dora made her way down the stairs. "Got to make the bread," she mumbled, waving her hand in front of her, trying to dispel the haze. She dragged her feet and finally pushed the door to the kitchen open. "Bread," she mumbled again, moving to the pantry. She pulled out various jars to set on the table.

Next, she went to the icebox. On the way there, the fog had cleared from her vision, and she saw the moonlight illuminating the side yard. "Is there someone out there?" She went to the back door and stared intently, trying to understand the scene before her.

A tall, dark-haired man seemed to be embracing a woman. "In our yard?" When she reached for the doorknob, she got a better view of the duo's embrace. The man's hands weren't on her face but wrapped around her neck! Dora pulled at the knob, but the door didn't budge. She banged on the window, trying to save the woman.

The man seemed not to hear her as he finished the job, and the woman dropped to the ground. He turned his eyes onto Dora and started toward her, his cape whipping in the wind.

She screamed, and the fog overcame her as she fell to the ground.

Voices penetrated the haze around her, but she felt frozen.

"Dora!"

"What's she doing down here?"

"I just left her for a moment."

"Let's move her upstairs."

She was being lifted and then everything went black.

"Drink this. Swallow, swallow."

Black eyes bored into hers. Dora swallowed, and her eyes closed.

CHAPTER 2

"Hot," Dora muttered and pushed off the covers.

"No, you have to keep them on," a soft voice said.

She felt the weight of the blankets return. She stopped struggling and fell back to sleep.

When she later awoke, she stretched. "Ow!"

"Dora, does something hurt?"

She opened her eyes slowly in the sunny room. She turned her head and found Tim and Emma sitting next to her. "Why are you both here? Did I oversleep?"

Emma put a shaky hand to her mouth. "She's herself."

"Of course I am. Why wouldn't I be?"

Tim put a hand to her forehead and said with a tired smile, "The fever's finally broken."

"Have I been sick?" Dora asked, trying to sit up.

"Let me help you," Tim said. He stood and moved her into a sitting position, while Emma moved to the other side of the bed to arrange her pillows.

"You got sick about three days ago," explained Emma.

"Three days! Did I miss Christmas?"

Emma laughed. "No, it's still a week away. You did try to help with the baking; we found you there this morning."

"I did?" She put a hand to her head. "I don't remember."

"You will. In time. The doctor said that it's very normal," Tim told her.

"When can I get up? There are so many things to do. The decorations will need to go up."

"Done and done," Emma assured her sister.

Dora picked at the blanket and asked dejectedly, "I haven't been missed?"

"Well, I've missed you," Tim said, kissing her cheek.

"It doesn't seem like it," she muttered. "Can I get up? I could use a bath."

"I'll help you." Tim picked her up and carried her to the bathroom. A little while later, she stood in her robe. She felt refreshed but still weak.

"Would you like to go back to bed?" he asked, watching her. Her hands were shaking, and she could barely stand.

"No, I'd like to move downstairs."

"And check to see if we put out the decorations where you want them," he said drolly.

"I want to be around everyone." *And check if everything's where I want them,* she admitted to herself.

"Oh, let her come downstairs," Emma said from the doorway.

"You'll watch her?" asked Tim.

"Oh, for goodness sake, just get me downstairs," Dora snapped.

Emma and Tim helped her get dressed, and Tim carried her downstairs. She reached out to the garland wrapped around the staircase. "It looks nice," she said softly.

Emma raised her eyebrows. "We can change anything you don't like."

They walked into the sitting room and sat her down in front

of the Christmas tree. "The tree isn't decorated!"

"We saved that for you," said Tim.

"Thank you." She put a hand to her chest, trying to pull herself together.

"It wasn't us; it was—" Emma started.

"Mama, Mama! You're up!" A little girl, about four years old with red hair, ran in and wrapped her arms around Dora's legs. "I made them wait! I told them you had to be here to decorate the tree!"

Dora teared up and bent down to hug her daughter. "My sweet girl, thank you."

"Lottie, we need to go Christmas shopping. Why not give Mama a break?" Tim asked.

"I'd just like to hold her for another moment," Dora said, holding Lottie tightly.

"Mama, too tight! Too tight!" Lottie struggled against her mother. Dora loosened her grip and let her stand back. "When can we decorate the tree?" Lottie demanded.

"Tonight," Dora told her.

"Why not in a few days?" suggested Emma. "You'll be less weak and able to participate."

"She's right," Tim agreed.

"Oh, okay," she gave in. "I'll make you a list of items I need."

"Awww," Lottie pouted.

"We'll decorate soon, I promise."

"Okay," she said.

"You do sound more like yourself," Emma teased her sister.

Tim got Dora some paper and a pencil. She took them and, while she was jotting down her items, Emma looked at her brother-in-law. "Tim, I have a package for Hen. Could you pick it up for me?"

"We should be able to handle that; just write down the location," Tim confirmed.

Emma pulled out her notebook, wrote quickly, tore off the

piece of paper, and handed it to him. "It's her dress for the Christmas dance."

Dora tore off her list and handed it to him. Tim looked at the two lists and studied them. "Hmm. We should still be able to get everything done. We'll just have to be quick about it."

"You started decorating for Christmas. Didn't you think I'd be better soon?" Dora asked Emma.

"I prayed you would be," Emma replied and took her hand.

"We need to get going," Tim said to Lottie.

Dora kissed her on the head and said, "Listen to Papa."

"I will, I promise," Lottie assured her.

"Go get ready," Tim told his daughter. She ran to the foyer, Tim following and helping her get on her coat, hat, and muffler. "We're going!" he called out.

"Be safe!" Dora called back.

"We will," he said and opened the door to go outside. The wind blew it out of his hand, and it slammed into the wall. "Watch out, Papa," Lottie scolded him, holding onto his hand tightly.

"Thanks," Tim said and walked them carefully out into the strong wind.

"Would you like me to get you anything?" Emma asked Dora. "Are you hungry?"

"No food just yet. A book would be nice."

She got one for Dora and moved back to her chair. Emma reached out to the table beside her and picked up her current lace project.

"What're you working on?" Dora asked, the book unopened in her lap.

"Lace for Henrietta's Christmas dress. She's going with a young man."

"That's nice. Is she nervous?"

Emma laughed. "Henrietta? No, she asked the boy."

"She's a strong girl."

"Knows what she wants," Emma confirmed.

"Emma," Dora said tentatively.

"Yes," Emma responded, absently looking down at her lacework.

"Emma!"

Emma looked up, concerned. "What's wrong? Are you feeling okay?"

"I think I saw something outside. When I was sick."

"Dora, the doctor said your high fever could've led to you seeing things that weren't there."

"I guess so. It just seemed so real," Dora muttered and opened her book to read.

Emma sighed and put down the lace. "What did you see?"

"A tall man with dark hair."

"What was he doing?"

"He was strangling a woman."

"Do you remember anything about her?"

"She had long, curly brown hair that shone in the moonlight."

"That's very detailed," Emma commented.

"Well, it was my first time witnessing a murder. I wanted to get it right," Dora said with a slight smile.

Emma frowned. The doctor had been sure it was the fever.

"You believe me, don't you?" Dora asked. She could see that Emma was skeptical.

"I don't not believe you. How about we ask the doctor to come by and check you out?" Emma said firmly.

"You mean reassure me," Dora grumbled.

"That too. Do you want to see him today?"

"No. I'd just like to be with family today."

"I think we can arrange that."

CHAPTER 3

"Hey," Jeremy said, walking into the kitchen.

Dora didn't respond. She stood staring intently out of the kitchen door.

"Hi, home for lunch?" Emma asked, lifting a cheek for a kiss.

"Is she doing better?" Jeremy asked in a low voice, walking over to get a cookie from the jar.

Emma didn't look up from the pastry dough she was rolling out. "She's been resting and taking her medicine. I thought she might want to do a little something in the kitchen to keep her busy."

"Is it working?"

"She's still fixating on that dream she had," she answered in the same tone.

"*Was* it just a dream?"

"The doctor said that a high fever might cause hallucinations," she reasoned. A cold breeze hit them. They looked at the door where Dora had stood.

"Dammit! Where is she?" Emma demanded, running to the door.

"You don't think she's outside?" Jeremy asked, moving to her side.

"Tim!" Emma yelled.

He ran into the room. "Why's the door open? Where's Dora?"

"Outside, we think!" Emma hollered over the noise of the wind. The three pushed out into the heavy snowfall.

"Do you see her?" yelled Tim.

"No," Emma replied.

"We need to split up!" shouted Jeremy over the wind.

"She can't have gotten far!" Emma yelled back. She gripped her arms over her chest against the cold, stumbling through the snow. "Dora!"

"Dora!" yelled Tim and Jeremy.

Emma fell face-first into the snow.

"Are you okay?" Jeremy called.

"I tripped on something." She struggled to her knees. "Wait, is that…" She started digging in the snow. It was a shoe. "It's Dora!" she yelled.

Tim and Jeremy ran over to help pull Dora out of the snow. Tim gathered her up, and they ran back inside. Jeremy pushed hard against the door to get it closed. He ran out of the kitchen door into the dining room.

"Ethyl!" Tim yelled to their cook. "Go get blankets, towels, and a nightgown," he ordered. She rushed out, the door swinging closed behind her.

Jeremy caught it and called from the doorway, "Bring her in here; the fireplace is the best place to warm her up."

Tim carried Dora's shivering body to the fireplace in the dining room. Jeremy stoked the fire until the flames leaped up and gave the room some warmth.

"We need to get these clothes off of her," Emma told him.

"I'll step out," Jeremy said, discreetly moving to the foyer. Emma and Tim unbuttoned Dora's shirt and removed it and her skirt. Ethyl ran in, her arms loaded with various articles. They dried her off and put her in the dry nightgown.

Ethyl said, "I brought these for you, too." She handed Tim and Emma towels to dry off.

"Jeremy," Emma called, "you can come in." He returned and took a towel to dry his hair and shirt.

They sat by the fire, drying off. Dora was cradled in Tim's arms. She moaned and opened her eyes.

"Dora, why'd you go outside?" asked Tim.

"I was looking for something."

"What?" Emma asked her.

"Nothing," Dora replied, her voice flat.

The three looked at each other. "Was it about what we discussed earlier?" Emma asked.

"You mean the hallucination?"

"That's what the doctor said."

"I've changed my mind; I want to talk to him today. I feel like I'm not seeing things clearly." Dora held a hand to her head. "I just feel so dizzy."

"We can talk to the doctor and see if he can come by," Tim said. "But you can't go back outside."

She stared at the flames and didn't say anything.

Emma took her hand and asked, "Do you want to talk about it?"

"I already have," Dora retorted.

"Yes, you have," Emma agreed. She was thinking about the details Dora had shared earlier. A tall man with dark hair. And a woman with long, curly brown hair.

Once Dora's hair was dry, Tim carried her upstairs. She could be heard loudly complaining all the way up.

"Any idea what that was about?" asked Jeremy.

"That little jaunt into the snow?" He nodded. "I think she was investigating."

"In the snow?"

"She feels strongly that what she saw was real. She must've been searching for something that'd prove he'd been outside."

"And if it was?"

"Then we have a murderer in our midst."

"Oh, good. Well, it is Christmas, and we do have a tradition to uphold."

"Murderous Christmas Mischief."

"Good title," Jeremy murmured.

CHAPTER 4

A little while later, Tim walked down the stairs. Emma walked out of the sitting room to meet him. "How is she?"

"Quiet. And I think a bit angry."

"Should I go to her?" she asked, her hand on the banister and her foot on the first step.

"She has Lottie with her; they're reading," he replied, rubbing a hand through his hair.

Jeremy joined them. "Let's move into the sitting room."

The three sat down. "What's our next move?" Emma asked them.

Tim sat back and considered. "Jeremy, can you get a note to the doctor?"

"Yes, I'll go over now. I'll also pick up Hen and Patrick from the bakery."

"Thanks, I'd forgotten," Tim said, laying his head back on the chair.

"Also get Hen's dress from the dressmaker," Emma said to Jeremy.

"I guess I'm not doing all that well with remembering things either," Tim said morosely.

"I'll take care of it." Jeremy went to get his coat.

They heard the door open and close.

"It'll get better," Emma told her brother-in-law.

"I know, I really do," said Tim.

"Dora's usually our rock. She's the one we all depend on."

"I know."

"We'll have to be that for her."

Tim straightened and said, "You're right." He got up and charged out of the room.

"Where're you going?" Emma asked and followed him into the foyer.

"To the kitchen, I have an idea that may cheer her up."

Emma shook her head, walked back, and picked up the lace to work on. It was some time later when she heard loud voices in the foyer. She walked out to greet Jeremy, Hen, and Patrick. Jeremy was carrying a big box. She ran over and got it. "Any problems?"

Hen had seen the box in the carriage and waited to ask about it "Is that my dress?"

"It is."

She clapped excitedly. "Can we try it on now?" she asked.

Tim walked out of the kitchen with Lottie. "Hello, everyone. Jeremy, did you deliver the note to the doctor?"

"I did. He says that he'll be over first thing tomorrow."

"He didn't have time tonight?"

"He's still with the Simpson kid."

"How is he?" asked Emma.

"The doctor says he's still critical," Jeremy replied.

"There've been so many people sick this year," Tim lamented.

"Same as last year," Jeremy agreed. "We could get the other doctor."

Tim shook his head. "No, I'd rather we go with Dr. Jones."

Hen reached out to touch the box.

"We'll work on it later," Emma told her.

"Will there be time for you to add the lace?" Hen asked, biting her lip.

"There's plenty of time, even if I have to stay up all night," she promised.

"Did I hear someone say dinner's ready?" a voice from the stairs softly questioned.

"Dora!" Tim ran over to her. "Are you feeling better?"

"I am." She looked at Tim, Jeremy, and Emma. "I'm sorry I worried everyone today."

"I'm just glad you're okay," Tim replied, brushing the hair off her face.

"Papa, you said it was dinner time," Lottie whined, pulling on his coat.

Everyone laughed.

Ethyl had put together a hearty stew, and they used the bread Emma had made earlier. The family pitched in and set the table. Ethyl and Jake walked out of the kitchen. Jake carried the large pot of stew, and Ethyl followed with pitchers of milk and water.

Emma got the bread and butter, and they sat down. Blessings were said, Tim filled each bowl, and they passed them around the table. The room was quiet, with the sounds of spoons scraping the bowls. The time passed, and at the end of dinner, the food was cleared away. Dora stood to help, and Tim stopped her. "Not tonight, please."

She smiled and said, "For you."

"Why don't you move into the sitting room, and I'll help Ethyl with dessert?" he asked.

Jeremy and Emma stood and escorted Dora and the kids to the sitting room. The kids sat on the floor; the older kids read, and Lottie played with her doll.

Tim walked in carrying a tray holding a pitcher and glasses. Ethyl came behind him, carrying the pastry.

"Ethyl, I didn't think you made apple strudel today," Dora told her, looking down at the apple-filled pastries.

"I didn't," she said and nodded to Tim.

"It was me," he acknowledged.

"You made these?" Dora asked with raised eyebrows.

"I know they're your favorite."

"Thank you," she said and kissed him. He handed her one as the group looked on. She took a bite. "Yum."

The group seemed more hesitant to take the pastry and try it. "I'll do it," said Emma bravely. She picked one up and took a bite; everyone watched. "It's very good," she exclaimed.

"You didn't trust me?" Dora asked her sister with a laugh.

"Well, you have to like them. You're married to him."

The rest of the group took the pastries and punch.

"Hey, you were waiting to see if it was any good?" Tim asked, holding a hand to his chest, feigning hurt.

Jeremy answered. "Well, Tim, you aren't known for your baking skills."

"That's true," he admitted. "I couldn't have done it without Ethyl's support."

"He did it all on his own. I just gave some notes," Ethyl said with a wink to Tim.

CHAPTER 5

*H*en tapped the table impatiently, her fingernails clattering. Jeremy looked at Emma. "I think someone wants you," he murmured under his breath.

She checked her watch. "I do need to head up and work on the dress."

"You might let her know," he suggested.

"Hen, would you like to go upstairs now?" Emma asked the girl.

She jumped up. "Yes, please."

"Take your plate to the kitchen first," Emma directed. Hen picked up her plate and went over to get Emma's. "Thank you."

Dora sat with Lottie in her lap, looking at the tree. Tim caught Emma's eye and nodded to Dora. She gave him a quick nod.

"Dora, would you like to join us? I'd like your assistance in the lace placement."

Dora looked up quickly and said, "Yes, I'd like that. Tim, can you take Lottie?"

He stood and went over to Lottie. "Come on, girlie, we can play together."

"Will you play dolly with me, Papa?" she asked.

He smiled. "Yes, I'll play dolly. First, I need to get Mama upstairs."

"I'll sit with her," Jeremy said.

"Good." Tim set Lottie on the carpet. "Uncle Jeremy says he'll play dolly with you."

"Wait, what?" Jeremy said.

Lottie walked over to him and took his hand. "Come on, Uncle Jeremy. Come play dolly with me."

"But… but…" Jeremy protested. He looked a bit helpless as Lottie led him out of the room.

"Well, I may just take a while upstairs," Tim murmured happily.

"Oh, you. You know you like to play dolly," Dora teased him.

He went to her chair, and she stood. She put a hand to her head. "Still dizzy?" he asked.

"A little, but I want to go help with the dress."

"Have you taken your medicine?"

"Just before dinner," she assured him.

"Good." He picked her up in his arms.

She protested. "I can walk by myself."

"If you want to go up, you'll be carried," Tim said firmly.

"Fine." She settled into his protective arms.

Emma and Hen went up the staircase. Tim followed closely behind them.

When they got to the room, Emma said, "Hen, get the dress hung on the form."

"You can set me down, Tim," Dora said.

He did as she asked. "Don't tire yourself out," he warned her.

"I won't." He left the room, and Dora sighed.

"Cut him some slack. He's trying," Emma commented, picking up her sewing kit.

"I know. I just don't like to feel so dependent."

"Emma! The dress," Hen begged.

"Sorry, Hen," Emma replied.

"That's right, let's get to work," Dora said.

Emma opened her sewing kit and took out the lace pieces; she'd started the project months earlier.

Hen ran over to see them. "They're so pretty!" she exclaimed.

"Take them over to the form and we'll start pinning them on."

Hen carried the pieces over to the form. Dora and Emma joined her and started to place the lace. Emma directed the final placement. They stepped back and looked at the finished product.

The green dress had a high neck, with fabric gathered into folds on the left shoulder; these were mimicked in the skirt with a gathered waist. The lace had been placed diagonally down the top and in rows down the bottom.

"Dying the lace black was a good choice. It goes well with the dark green," said Dora.

"It's lovely," Hen agreed, reaching out to touch it. "I can't wait to wear it."

"You'll have to wait. I have a lot of sewing to do," Emma cautioned her. She checked her watch and saw she'd get little sleep that night.

"I want to help," Dora said.

"Me too," Hen added.

Emma had worked with Hen on her sewing, but she still cautioned the girl. "Be sure to use small stitches."

"I will," Hen promised.

They sat on one of the twin beds with the dress laid out between them. The room grew quiet as each concentrated on their sewing.

"Are you feeling less dizzy?" Emma asked Dora.

"I'm better; it comes and goes." They worked for a few hours and stopped when a knock sounded on the door. Jeremy walked in.

"It's time for Hen to go to bed."

Tim was behind him. "You too, Dora. You're still recovering."

"But I don't want to leave all the work for Emma," Dora protested.

"You go ahead. I've got it," Emma assured her.

"There's so much to do," Dora said, touching the dress.

"I'll finish up tonight and then we can see if I missed anything tomorrow."

"I'll come back and check on you after Hen goes to bed," Jeremy said to Emma. He looked at Hen. "It's a big day tomorrow, and you need to get some rest."

She touched the dress and nodded. "Thank you, Emma and Dora," she said and kissed both on the cheek. "Goodnight."

"Night, dear," Emma told her. Jeremy and Hen left to head downstairs to her room.

Tim walked over to Dora. She put out her hand to stop him. "I can walk down."

He started to argue, but saw that she seemed steadier. "Okay," he said and offered her his arm. She took it and they left the room.

Emma took the dress and moved to the heavy stuffed chair near the east window. She'd completed the top portion and started working where Dora had stopped.

"Tall man, dark hair," she murmured. *That could be many people,* she thought. She set her sewing down and looked out the large window. The view was of the house next door. She absently counted the windows and saw that two windows on the third floor had lights illuminating them. "Oops, the curtains are open," she murmured. A woman walked by, and she had long, brown curly hair.

Jeremy walked in. "Taking a break?"

"Hmm." She didn't turn away from the window. "Jeremy, that doctor who was here last night..."

"Yes?" he said, taking off his jacket and rolling up his sleeves.

"Didn't Tim say he lived next door?"

Jeremy walked over and stood behind her. "Yeah," he said, "right there."

"Dora's description of the murderer somewhat matches that of the doctor."

"Well, that kind of makes sense. She might have incorporated him into her hallucinations."

"Yeah, but this afternoon she told me the woman he murdered had long, brown curly hair." She tapped the window.

He looked and saw what she saw. He frowned. "They do match the descriptions, but she's obviously alive. It must be the illness. You saw her at dinner tonight. She's still recovering."

"That might be." She picked up the needle and started to sew. Jeremy sat in the chair opposite her and opened the book he'd brought with him.

A long time later, Emma moved over to the sleeping Jeremy. "Jeremy," she said softly. He snorted in his sleep. "Jeremy," she nudged his shoulder, "we need to get to bed."

"What time is it?"

"Three am. Come on, time for bed."

They changed into their nightclothes and climbed into bed. "Morning's gonna come fast tomorrow," he said with a yawn.

CHAPTER 6

The next morning, the bell rang, telling them breakfast was on the table. This time, Jeremy nudged Emma. "Up and at 'em. Breakfast."

"Ugh. Too soon," she moaned, putting her face in the pillow.

"Stay in bed. I'll tell them to hold breakfast."

She lifted her head. "Oh, that'll go over just great with Dora. She'll march up here and drag me downstairs. I have to get up anyway. I still have some work to do on Hen's dress."

"I thought you finished last night."

"Almost. I had to stop, or I was going to make mistakes. I was starting to get cross-eyed."

Jeremy kissed her cheek. "I'll meet you on the other side." He got out of bed, walked to the bookcase, and pulled it open.

She stood, grabbed a hairbrush, and began pulling it through her long hair as she tried to keep her eyes open. She pulled on her robe and walked down to the bathroom to splash water on her face. After her teeth were brushed and her face washed, she felt more able to face the day. On the way back to her room, she saw Dora on the landing. "Were you looking for me?" Emma called over.

Dora cocked her head and said, "No, I came up for something."

"Can I help?"

"No, no. I'm okay." Dora turned and started back down the stairs.

Well, that was odd, Emma thought. She dressed quickly and pulled her hair into a bun on the back of her head.

She heard a tap, tap on the door. "On my way," she called. She put the final pin in her hair and went to open the door. Hen stood there, and Emma did a quick check over her shoulder to make sure the bookshelf was closed. It was. *Whew,* thought Emma. They weren't ready for Hen to know about her and Jeremy's "arrangement".

"Is the dress finished?" Hen asked breathlessly.

"Well, good morning to you, too, Hen," chided Emma.

"Good morning, Emma," she responded. "Is the dress finished?"

"Just about. You can come up after breakfast. We need to redo a few things."

"Were my stitches too long?"

"A few of them," Emma admitted. "We want everything secured. I also want to check those last stitches I did; I'm pretty sure those need to be redone."

"Okay. Ready for breakfast?"

"I am."

"So am I," Jeremy said from his doorway. He walked toward them, pulling on his jacket. The three headed down together.

They joined the rest of the family, helping to set the table and carry in the food. Once they were settled, everyone filled their plates.

"Dora, the doctor will be here this morning," Tim told his wife.

She put down her fork. "I'm better." He didn't look at her

and continued to add jam to Lottie's toast. "You don't believe me about what I saw, so I must still be sick," she accused him.

"You were dizzy this morning," he reminded her. "And you said you wanted to see him today."

Emma added, "You asked for him yesterday, don't you remember?"

Dora rubbed her head; she'd been so confused lately.

"Dora, for me?" implored Tim. "I want to make sure you're recovering. And we need to make sure the chill you got yesterday doesn't bring the illness back on."

She picked up her fork. "Fine, I'll see him."

They heard knocking at the front door. "That should be him now," Tim said.

"I'll let him in," Jeremy said. He got up to go greet the doctor. They entered the dining room together.

Dora frowned. "Good morning, Dr. Phillips. Can I at least finish my breakfast?" she asked.

The doctor chuckled. "Only if you offer me something to eat."

"Tim, pass the trays to the good doctor," Dora ordered.

Dr. Phillips chuckled again. "Please, I was up all night again." Tim moved the trays closer to him. He took a plate and helped himself.

"How is Sam?" Emma asked him.

"He made it through," Dr. Phillips mumbled with his mouth full of a biscuit, "and the fever broke."

"That's good," Emma replied and the others nodded. Breakfast continued at a slow pace.

When they were done, the group got up and carried their dishes to the kitchen, leaving Dora and Dr. Phillips alone. He put down his napkin and asked, "Can I get your exam started now?"

"Yes, I think it's time." She stood and had to brace her hand on the table. The world spun around her.

The doctor walked over to her. "Has this been going on for a while?"

She shook her head. "Just since I woke up from the fever."

"Take my arm. Where would you be most comfortable?"

"The study." She took his arm and pointed to the left.

"Hang on to me," he said, patting her hand.

They made their way slowly to the room. He helped her to the desk chair and went back to close the door. He opened his bag and pulled out his stethoscope and a small depressor. "Now, open wide," he said as he walked over to her.

She did as requested as he took her pulse and placed the stethoscope to monitor her heartbeat. "Dr. Phillips, what was wrong with me?"

"The flu. It's been everywhere. Half the city has it. I haven't slept in days."

"I appreciate you coming to see me."

"I finally had some time."

"No, I mean a few days ago."

The doctor stood and put his stethoscope into his bag. He retrieved a bottle and returned to her. "Oh, that wasn't me."

"What do you mean?" she stuttered. "Who was it then?"

"Tim sent me a note that a doctor had moved in next door."

"He didn't mention that," she said, putting a hand to her head. "At least, I don't think he did. I've been so forgetful."

"It may have slipped his mind."

"Yes, it's been a busy few days." Dora looked down and picked at her skirt. Finally, she said, "Doctor, would I have seen things that weren't there?"

"When your fever was high, you could've had hallucinations," he confirmed.

"Would they have been vivid, like I could touch them?" she asked.

"In some cases," he conceded.

"It just seemed so real. I guess I need to try to forget it."

"Put it out of your mind, my dear. The holidays are here, enjoy them."

"I'll try."

Tim stuck his head in. "I brought your medicine in case the doctor needs to see it."

Dr. Phillips walked over and took the bottle. "Thank you, Tim."

"Let me know if you need anything," he said, starting to pull the door closed.

"Tim," called Dora, "you can stay."

"I will if you want me to."

She held out her hand to him. "Please."

He walked over and took her hand. They both watched the doctor.

Dr. Phillips studied the bottle. "When did the dizziness start?" he asked with a frown.

"I've been dizzy off and on since I woke up from the fever," Dora replied.

"How often have you been taking this medication?" he asked, tapping the bottle.

"At least twice a day," Tim said, "per the other doctor's instructions."

The doctor opened the bottle and poured some of the contents onto his finger. First, he smelled it, then put it to his tongue. "That's what I thought. Opium."

"That isn't a normal treatment?" Tim asked, frowning.

"It can be, but Dora's reaction to the opium tells me it's too strong for her."

"Could that cause the hallucination to come back?" she asked tentatively.

"Yes, it might."

"Is there something else I can take?"

"Yes, I'll give you quinine sulfate for chills and fever. Only use it if the fever comes back. For now, what you need is to stay out of the snow. We need you warm and rested."

"They told you about that?" Her cheeks turned red.

"Yes. Will you listen and stay inside?"

"Yes, doctor," she said, her head bowed.

Dr. Phillips raised her chin. "We don't want a relapse."

"Dora?" Tim prompted her.

"I'll do my best," she said.

"That's all we can ask." Dr. Phillips continued to hold the bottle. "Would you mind if I took this with me?"

"Take it," Dora said. "If that's what's making me dizzy and see things that aren't there, then I don't want it. Will I feel better now?"

"Once the drug's out of your system, you should be fine. I need to get back to my unhealthy patients," he teased. "Merry Christmas, Dora and Tim."

"Thank you, doctor. You too."

After the doctor left, Tim knelt next to Dora. "Are you feeling better?"

"Yes, I feel a bit silly now. You were right, I did need to see the doctor." Black eyes flashed in front of her. She shook her head to dispel the image.

They walked out of the room together, feeling the cold air from the open door as Dr. Phillips left, and continued into the sitting room. The kids were all there with Emma.

Emma saw them. "What did he say?" she asked.

Dora and Tim walked over and sat down on the settee. "I was taking too much medication."

"Is that what..." she trailed off.

"Caused the visions? He said it's possible."

The room went quiet after that statement.

"Emma?" Hen asked.

"Yes?" Emma knew what she would say next.

"Can we work on my dress?"

"You mean the one for the party tonight?" Emma teased her.

"Yes, please."

Emma stood and said, "Let's go up to the sewing room."

Hen clapped and started at a run toward the stairs.

"Emma, try to get some rest when you finish," Jeremy called to her.

"I'll try," she said as she followed Hen up the stairs at a slower pace.

When they got to the fourth floor, Hen could see that the dress had been placed back on the form. "Oh, Emma, it's so lovely," she squealed.

"We still have work to do," Emma cautioned.

"Show me."

Emma took the dress off the form and carried it to the bed. "Come look at some of these stitches."

Hen walked over and concentrated on the dress. "These are yours," Emma pointed out. "Now look at Dora's stitches and mine. Tell me what you see."

"Mine are too wide."

"Yes, and eventually they could catch on to something and pull the lace off."

"We need to fix it."

"We do." Emma took a small set of scissors from her sewing kit and snipped the loose threads.

As she was removing them, Hen asked nervously, "Emma, can I try to fix it?"

Emma smiled. Hen was independent and wanted to try things for herself. "Start there." She pointed.

"Here?"

"Yes."

Hen started on the stitching and focused intently on her work. A little while later, she asked, "Emma, can you check my stitches?"

"I can." She looked over and saw that Hen had listened, and

the stitches mimicked hers and Dora's. "That's very good. Keep up with that. Do you want me to help?"

"I can do it on my own."

"I'll lie here then. Let me know if you need me." Emma stretched out on the bed and closed her eyes.

"Emma, time to get up," Hen said later, gently shaking her.

Emma shook her head and rubbed her eyes. "Do you need some help?"

"I'm finished. Can you check it?"

She sat up and moved to the side of the bed. Hen set the garment in her lap. She looked down at the stitches. "You finished! How long was I asleep?"

"A couple of hours."

"You've been working all this time?"

"Yes. Is it okay? I don't want to accidentally ruin it at the party."

Emma examined all of Hen's work and said, "You did a wonderful job. I'm so proud of you." She grabbed her in a hug.

Hen put her head on Emma's shoulder and hugged her back. "Is it done now?"

"Almost," Emma told her. "Would you like to try it on?"

Hen grinned. "I'd love to." She put on the dress and moved to stand on a wooden box in the middle of the room. Emma moved to button her up and got out a folding wooden carpenter's ruler. She walked around the skirt to check the hem of the dress.

"Is it even?" Hen asked, bending over to see what Emma was doing.

"Baby, you need to stand still." Hen straightened and waited. "It's fine."

"What're you doing now?"

"I'm checking the gathering." She stepped back. "I think it's ready for tonight."

"Oh, Emma, I can't wait for the party to start." They heard

the dinner bell ring. "Lunch," Hen stated and started to charge out.

Where has the day gone? Emma thought. "Hey, aren't you forgetting something?" she asked with a raised eyebrow.

"Oh, this?" Hen asked, twirling around the room. "I thought I might keep it on forever." Emma pointed to the dress stand. "Oh, all right." She went to stand by Emma so she could unbutton it for her. She pulled on her dress while Emma settled the party dress back onto the form.

The bell rang again.

Hen ran to the door and stopped. "Are you coming down?"

"On my way," Emma responded, following her down.

Jeremy met them halfway. "I was just on my way to get you two."

"We heard the bell," Hen said and continued quickly down the stairs.

"How're you feeling?" Jeremy asked Emma.

"Great, actually."

"You do look more rested. How'd that happen?"

"Hen finished the dress while I napped."

"Wow."

"Wait until you see her in it."

"It isn't her I'm worried about; it's the boy she's going with," he muttered.

"Your little girl's growing up," Emma told him as she kissed his cheek.

CHAPTER 7

fter dinner, Emma buttoned the dress up and told Henrietta to turn around. It was the final fitting before the party, and Emma was doing a final check on the dress.

Henrietta whirled around, and the green skirt swept the floor. She ran over to the mirror and gasped. "Oh, Emma, it's so lovely."

"You're lovely in it. What's the boy like?"

"Jimmy," Hen said, admiring herself in the mirror, "is very nice looking."

Emma laughed. "That's all you know about him? When did you meet him?"

"We used to go to the same school."

"St. Michael's?"

"No, before that, when I lived with the other people." Hen called her parents 'other people'. Emma didn't correct her; her parents had abused and then abandoned the girl.

"Is he still in school?"

"No, he had to go to work." Hen walked over to Emma and grabbed her hands. "Emma, I wanted to ask you something."

"Go ahead," she said, walking over to sit down on one of the two twin beds set up in the sewing room. "Sit with me," Emma said and patted the bed next to her.

"Jimmy needs somewhere to live, and I was thinking about Mrs. Spencer's boarding house."

Emma frowned. "Where does he live now?"

"I think he's sleeping wherever he can find a place. And you don't have to worry; he's working now, so he has money to pay for his room."

Emma mulled that over and drummed her fingers on her lips. "We do have an opening. Jimmy will need to meet with Tim and Dora before we can make that decision."

"Oh, that's wonderful."

"Let's take off the dress and get it hung up."

"Do I have to?" Hen asked. "It's so pretty."

"The dance is tonight; you'll have plenty of opportunity to wear it."

"Okay."

"Come here. Let me help you take it off."

Henrietta walked over and turned her back so that Emma could unbutton the dress. She slipped it off and handed it to Emma to hang up.

Dora asked from the doorway, "What're we doing with your hair?"

"My hair? I don't know. What should I do?" Henreitta asked, touching it.

Dora walked around her, scrutinizing Hen's hair. "How about some curls, and we put it up?"

Hen clapped. "Yes, please."

"Well, sit down."

She sat at the small dressing table. "Can I wear some make-up?" she asked, tentatively touching the items laid out on the small table.

"I think some rouge, face powder, and lip salve should work. What do you think, sister?" Dora asked.

"Just for the party, though," Emma responded.

Hen nodded.

"Hair first?" Emma asked, touching Hen's head lightly.

"We'll need to move to the kitchen," Dora replied.

"Let's go."

They stopped by Dora's room to get a curling iron, and then they headed down to the kitchen. They waved at the men as they walked by the sitting room. Lottie got up to join them.

"Lottie, stay here with us," Tim told the little girl.

"Awww, I want to watch Hen get pretty."

"Will you stay out of the way?"

"I will, Papa."

"If Mama tells you to come back, don't argue," Tim warned.

"Yes, Papa." She ran off.

"Finally, the girls are all gone," Patrick muttered.

"One day, Patrick, you'll want them around more." Jeremy laughed.

"Yeah, yeah," he said and went back to reading his book.

Lottie charged into the kitchen.

Ethyl ran over to her. "Don't get too close."

"I want to watch. Papa said I could as long as I listened to Mama."

"That's fine, Ethyl," Dora told the cook. "Put her in a chair over here."

Ethyl moved her to a chair near Dora. She sat, and Dora said, "Don't move; this is hot."

"Okay, Mama."

Hen sat, and Emma started brushing out her hair. "What do you think, curl all of it?" she asked Dora.

"No, it's thick and will look nice in a bun," Dora told her, holding Hen's hair up.

"Curl the top?"

"And around her face," Dora agreed. She pulled Hen's hair into a loose bun, leaving free hair on the sides and top.

Next, they started with the cooling iron, heating it on the stove and wrapping Hen's hair around it. They worked in sections until all the curls were pinned. They would stay pinned until she got dressed. They finished, and Lottie yelled, "Now do me!"

"I don't know, sweetie," Dora told her daughter.

Hen said, "We have time, if you want to curl her hair."

Dora went over to walk Lottie to the chair at the stove. "The iron's hot, and if you move too much, you might get burned."

"Like the stove?"

"Yes, like the stove. Will you hold still?"

"I will," she promised.

"Watch her," Emma mouthed at her sister. Dora nodded. Hen stayed, and Ethyl walked over to suggest different things for Lottie's hair. They decided on putting it up in a ponytail and curling the ends.

"How do I look?" Lottie asked excitedly.

"Very pretty," Hen told her.

"Let me see! Let me see!" Lottie demanded. Dora handed her the mirror. "I look like Hen." She giggled.

"Yes, just like me," Hen agreed. "Do you want to come with us to help me get dressed?"

"Yes!"

Hen took the little girl's hand, and they walked out into the foyer. Tim, Jeremy, and Patrick saw them walk by.

"I'm going to get dressed," Hen called to them.

"Ethyl, you can head home if you want," Dora offered.

The cook came out of the kitchen. "I told Jake I'd wait for him. He's over at the museum tonight. I would like to see Hen all dressed up."

"We should be down in a little while," Emma told her. The women moved upstairs.

When they were back in the sewing room, Hen asked, "Who'll meet Jimmy at the door?"

"Jeremy and Tim," Emma replied.

"Oh, gosh," Hen said slowly.

They paused, and Dora said, "I'm afraid your young man's in for an interview."

"More like an interrogation," said Emma. She looked at Hen. "Think Jimmy can get through it?"

Hen considered that and said, "Yeah, I think he can."

"You're going to need to practice walking down the stairs," Emma told her.

"Why? Is it because of the shoes?" Henrietta was wearing higher heels than she was used to.

"No, it's that you want to make an entrance," Emma clarified.

"A grand entrance," agreed Dora.

"An entrance," Hen repeated dreamily.

"And you want to wow the crowd," Emma said. She checked her watch. "It's time to put on your makeup."

"Not the dress?"

"The dress will be last."

Hen sat down on the chair, and Emma picked up the blush to add to Hen's cheeks. When she finished, Dora used a powder puff to dust her face. "Now, your lips," she said. She painted a little rouge and then brushed the salve across her lips.

Emma started to take the pins out of her hair and adjusted the curls on top of her head. She loosened some to cascade around her face.

Hen looked in the mirror and frowned. "It doesn't look like me."

Emma hugged her shoulder. "It is you, just a little more glamorous than usual."

"Now, the dress," said Dora. She got the dress from the form and put it over her arm. Emma helped Hen out of the dress she was wearing and laid it on the bed. They lowered the party dress to the ground, so she could step into it. Dora and Emma helped pull it up and secured it in place. Dora took care of the buttons while Emma carried over her shoes and helped Hen put them on.

"How do I walk down?" she asked.

"Slowly," Emma told her. Hen practiced walking across the floor. "Yes, that's exactly right," said Emma. Dora nodded in agreement.

CHAPTER 8

Tim shuffled a deck of cards and dealt them to Patrick, Jeremy, and himself.

"The boy should be here soon," Jeremy remarked, looking at his cards and throwing a chip into the pile.

"Two cards," said Patrick.

Tim asked him, "Do you know this boy?"

"I've seen him around," he said, taking the two cards from Tim.

"No comments?" Jeremy asked.

"Nah. He has an odd way of talking, though."

"What do you mean?"

They heard knocking on the door. "You'll see," Patrick muttered, dropping his cards on the table.

Emma walked downstairs with Dora. "Is that him?" she asked.

"Don't know," Jeremy replied from the dining table.

"You planning to let him in?" Emma asked, hands on her hips.

"I was thinking about leaving him out there," he said, not making a move from his spot.

"Come on." Another knock sounded. "Hen's excited about this."

"All right, fine," he said, throwing his cards on the table. He stood, strode to the door, and opened it.

A young man stood there, leaning on the doorframe. Jeremy's eyes narrowed.

"Henrietta here?" the young man asked.

"She might be, why?" Jeremy stayed where he was, blocking the entrance to the house.

Emma walked over to them and said, "Jeremy, let him in the house. It's freezing out there."

He finally stepped back and let him into the foyer.

The young man walked in and looked around. "You must be a lally-cooler," he said, walking over to the sitting room.

"What the hell did he say?" Jeremy muttered to Emma. "Is he speaking English?"

"Told you," Patrick said. "He says it's a nice place."

Tim walked closer and towered over the boy. "What's your name, son?"

Jimmy looked up and grinned. "Jimmy, sir. Jimmy MacDonald." He stuck out his hand, and Jeremy, Emma, and Tim shook it.

Just then, Henrietta appeared at the top of the stairs. Jimmy saw her and called up, "Chuckaboo!"

Emma looked at Jeremy. "Chuckaboo?" he muttered. She hid her smile behind her hand.

Hen grinned and walked down slowly. Dora nudged Emma. Emma nudged back. The girl was creating her entrance.

"She looks like a queen," Ethyl said, wiping tears from her eyes from the sitting room doorway.

Tim continued to tower over Jimmy. "What does your family do, young man?" Jeremy looked unmovable with his arms crossed over his chest. Patrick stayed back and squinted at Jimmy.

Jimmy didn't seem to be able to take his eyes off of Hen and asked absently, "What?"

Tim wouldn't let it go. "Young man, I'm talking to you."

"Just a sec," Jimmy said and ran over to greet Hen at the bottom of the steps.

"Hi," she greeted him shyly.

"Hey, chuckaboo, I got you a flower."

"You did?"

He reached into his jacket pocket, pulled out a small flower, and handed it to her. "You're the jammiest bits of jam," he said.

She took it and smiled. "Thank you."

"You're welcome." Jimmy offered her his arm, and they walked closer to the family. "My pops is shinning around and when he's not he's arf'arf'an'arf." He tilted his hand showing a drinking motion.

Jeremy shook his head in confusion. He had no idea what Jimmy had just said. "You need to come home right after the dance," he warned.

"But I'm sixteen," Hen protested. "The other kids want to hang out after."

"We won't wake snakes," Jimmy promised.

"What does that mean?" asked Jeremy, his voice showing his exasperation.

"It means we won't be getting into mischief," explained Hen.

"Jeremy, I think we can be flexible tonight," Emma said.

Patrick went to the closet and got Hen's coat and hat. "Thanks, Patrick," she said, pulling them on.

Tim walked over to the window. "It's started to snow again. I'll get the wagon," he said, going to get his coat.

"No, I have a carriage," Jimmy told him.

"Where did you get a carriage?" Tim asked dubiously, eyeing the boy.

"My boss told me I could use it."

"Where do you work?" Emma asked Jimmy.

"He works next door," volunteered Hen.

"With the doctor?" Dora asked, moving closer to Jimmy. "How long have you worked there?"

Tim looked at the snow outside. "There isn't time for any more questions. They need to get moving; the horse shouldn't be out in the weather that long."

"She'll be housed in a barn while we're at the dance," Jimmy assured them. They started to leave. Jimmy whispered to Hen.

She nodded and turned back to the group. "He's looking for a place to live. I told him that Dora and Tim would talk to him."

"You don't live with your parents?" Dora asked him.

"Arf'arf'an'arf," he said, mimicking drinking.

"Oh, right," said Dora. "Come by tomorrow and we can check if we have any openings."

"I'll meet you here," he promised

The two bundled up and walked quickly out of the house and down the stoop. The family watched from the door as Jimmy helped Henrietta up on the box and swung her into the carriage.

"Have fun," Emma called out. They watched them drive off in the carriage. "He seems like a nice boy," she said.

"What the hell was he talking about?" asked Jeremy. "I didn't understand most of what he said."

"It was slang, Uncle Jeremy," Patrick explained. "He uses it all the time."

"And you understood it?"

"Yeah, I got most of it."

"Yeah, well, I'm still not sure about him," Jeremy groused.

"You wouldn't be sure about anyone dating Hen," Emma remarked.

"That's true. How did sixteen get here so quickly?"

"If you remember, we met at that age," she reminded him.

"Yeah, and you had a knife at my throat."

"I still have it," she said with a smile.

He waggled his eyebrows at her. "You'll have to show me later."

"Oh, blech." Patrick moaned in disgust.

Emma and Jeremy laughed at him. "Dora, why'd you tell Jimmy to come by and see if we have an opening?" Tim asked her.

"We do have a few right now. That young couple has moved into their new house."

"One's a family room, and the other's a single," he reminded her.

"I thought I'd show him both."

"I'm sure he can only afford the single," Jeremy said.

"Well, we'll see, shall we?"

Emma watched her sister closely. *Was she still investigating?*

"Well, I don't like him. He's too high for his nut," Patrick said and walked off.

"Any idea what he meant by that?" Jeremy asked.

"None. Patrick, what does that mean?" Tim said, following his son down the hall.

CHAPTER 9

*J*immy and Hen arrived at the party, and he helped her with her coat. "The band's swinging tonight," he said.

"It is," she said, tapping her foot on the floor.

"Your new fam seems good."

"Yeah, I was lucky. Are you okay for now? Do you have someplace to sleep tonight?"

"I'm stayin' with friends, but a more permanent place would be nice. You want to dance?"

"I thought you'd never ask," she said with a grin.

He grabbed her hand and pulled her onto the dance floor.

"Are you coming to bed?" Emma asked Jeremy from the stairs. She was in her nightgown, and her hair hung down her back.

He stopped his pacing in front of the door. "She isn't home, and the snow's worse than when they left."

"She's a responsible girl."

"I'm not worried about her," he grumbled, moving to look out the window.

"I can tell," she murmured. "Jimmy seems nice."

He grumbled again.

"She's growing up, and I don't expect her to marry Jimmy."

"You don't?" he asked hopefully.

"No, he's just someone she has a crush on. Let it work itself out."

"It's getting late; maybe I should go look for them."

She checked the time and laughed. "Babe, the dance has barely ended. Give them some time."

"Well…" he began.

At that moment, the door swung open and Hen entered. "Bye," she called. She was humming and saw them standing in front of her. "The other kids decided it was better to go home, and Jimmy wanted to get the horse back to its stable." She took off her coat and hat and asked, "Were you waiting up?"

"Yes," started Jeremy.

"No," Emma said with a glare at Jeremy.

"Yes and no. Hmm."

"Did you have a good time?" asked Emma.

"Yeah," Hen said dreamily. She spun around in her dress. "Everyone said nice things about my dress, and we danced and danced. I could have danced all night. He just makes my heart jump."

"Why don't you head upstairs? I'll join you and help you with the dress."

"Oh, do I have to?" she asked.

Emma laughed. "Do you want to sleep in the dress?"

"I just don't want the night to end."

"Go on. We need to get it hung up." Emma watched Hen slowly make her way up the stairs. Jeremy walked over and put his arms around her. "Feeling old?" she asked.

"A little," he admitted.

"You still make my heart jump."

"Hmm, I'll have to do something about that," he said and lowered his head to kiss her.

After a few minutes, she said softly, "After I get Hen to bed."

CHAPTER 11

Tim opened his eyes and saw Dora standing at the window. The moonlight illuminated her white nightgown.

"How're you feeling?" he asked softly.

"Better," she said, still staring out the window.

"No more dizziness?"

"No. Tim, what do you know about the doctor next door?"

He yawned as he tried to order his thoughts. "Just that he moved to town about two weeks ago."

"How did you meet him?"

"Don't you remember?"

She shook her head. "Things are still a little fuzzy. I must've started getting sick around that time."

"You sent me over with cookies to welcome him and his wife."

"Did you see anything while you were there?"

He frowned. "I'm not sure what you mean."

She moved to the bed and sat next to him. "Does he have large hands and black eyes?"

"He did," he said cautiously. "Are you remembering him being here?"

"I think so," she said shortly. She'd remembered him here in this room, and that he'd been holding a pillow over her face. The man had tried to kill her.

CHAPTER 12

The next morning, Dora entered the kitchen and reached for her apron. Ethyl was already there, cutting bread to make toast. "Good morning. I'll start the eggs," Dora told her. She went to get the pan and placed it on the stove. She and Ethyl worked together quietly.

Jake pushed open the door and placed his camera on the table.

"Not there," Ethyl said.

"Oh, okay." He picked it back up.

"Put it over there, under the cabinet." She pointed. "Are you going out today?"

"Tony asked me to get some pictures together for a show."

Ethyl and Dora stopped what they were doing. "That's wonderful!" Dora beamed.

Ethyl walked over and took his hand. "I'm so proud of you."

His face reddened. "Would you like to help me with some pictures today?"

Ethyl glanced over at Dora. "Of course you can go," Dora told her. "We'll have sandwiches for lunch."

"What about dinner?" she asked.

"Well, Tim proved last night he can help in the kitchen. I'll put him to work."

Ethyl laughed. "He does take direction well." Dora laughed with her.

Breakfast was put on the table, Ethyl rang the bell, and the table was filled with people.

Tim was busy cutting up fruit for Lottie. "Biscuits, please," she said.

Dora got her one and put butter and jam on it. She cut it in half and handed it to her. "Tim, Ethyl needs some time off to help Jake with a project. And since you've proven to be such a good assistant, you can help me in the kitchen today."

He opened his mouth and closed it.

"No good deed…" Emma teased her brother-in-law.

"Uh, I do have to get the checks out today," he said. "People will want their pay and bonuses before Christmas break."

"We'll do sandwiches for lunch," Dora replied, "which will give you this morning. But I'll need help with dinner."

"I can help," Emma offered.

Tim looked relieved until Dora said, "No, I think Tim's shown he has skills we need to develop further."

"I guess I'm in," he grumbled.

"Oh, don't look so disappointed," chided Dora. "I'll make something sweet, and you can lick the bowl."

He smiled. "Now that's a good reason to be in the kitchen."

"What time are Patrick and Henrietta off?" Jeremy asked.

"Eleven, they worked the early shift this morning," Dora told him.

"There are a lot of parties that Cousin needed help with," said Emma.

"I'll pick them up on the way home," he said. "I need to go to the office for a few hours."

"Sister, Hen asked me to remind you that Jimmy said he could come over at lunch," Emma said.

"I'll be here."

"Invite him to lunch," suggested Emma.

Dora frowned. "Why?"

"Hen said that Jimmy was stuffing his pockets with food at the party, and she wasn't sure where he was going to sleep last night."

"I'll make sure that he eats," she assured her sister. "Do we want to decorate the tree tonight?"

"Yes, yes!" Lottie exclaimed, clapping her hands.

"Are you sure you're strong enough, Dora?" asked Tim.

"I'll rest this afternoon," she promised.

"I'll make sure you do."

"Jeremy, wait for me. I'll ride in with you," Emma said.

"You won't be here?" Dora asked her.

"I'm going to Mr. Pennington's office."

"I thought they were on break."

"They are, but Ethan has something he wants to review with me."

Ethyl brought out more toast from the kitchen. "I'll be back to help out with the tree decorating tonight," she told everyone.

"Thank you, Ethyl," Dora said. "Jeremy, I sent a cookie and pie order over to Cousin's this morning. Can you pick them up?"

The mood in the room lightened with that comment. Dora was definitely feeling better; she had her management hat on again. Everyone was being assigned their tasks for the day.

"I'll pick up the order when I get the kids," Jeremy confirmed.

"And me," Emma reminded him.

"And you," he confirmed.

"Tell us about the dance. Did Henrietta have a good time?" asked Dora.

"She was floating when she got home. I had trouble getting her to take off the dress."

"Did Jimmy have a good time?"

"Hen said yes, and they have another party they were invited to attend."

"Oh yeah? When?" Jeremy asked.

"New Year's Eve."

He frowned and didn't stop eating. Emma reached over and squeezed his hand. He just kept eating.

"Dance, dance," Lottie sang.

CHAPTER 13

*H*en entered the house in a rush. "Is he here?" she called as she struggled to remove her muffler, hat, and coat. Emma, Patrick, and Jeremy followed at a slower pace, carrying in boxes of cookies and pastries for the Christmas trimming.

Dora walked out of the sitting room with Lottie. "Take the boxes to the kitchen, please." The trio took the boxes where she directed.

Hen walked over to Lottie and ruffled her hair. "Hey, kid."

"Hi, Hen. Wanna play?"

"Soon, okay?"

"I expect Jimmy will be here soon," Jeremy told her, walking out of the dining room with Emma. He helped her take off her coat and pulled off his jacket and scarf.

"Lunch soon?" Patrick asked. He stood in the dining room doorway, chewing on a bit of apple.

"Put your coat in the closet," Dora told him.

They heard knocking on the door.

"He must've been watching for her," muttered Jeremy.

Hen grinned and ran to the door to let him in.

Jeremy moved in front of her. "Wait over there. I'll greet the boy." He went to the door and pulled it open.

"Is Henrietta home?" Jimmy asked, trying to see over Jeremy's shoulders.

"I think you know she is," he commented, not moving.

"Yeah, I was watching for her," he admitted.

Hen ran over and ducked under Jeremy's arm.

"Chuckaboo," he said with a grin.

"Hey."

"Jeremy," called Emma, "it's getting cold."

He grudgingly moved to let the boy in and shut the door.

The delay didn't affect Jimmy, and he rushed in to take Hen's hand.

Jeremy stepped between them again.

"Jeremy, why don't you come help me get the sandwich stuff out?" called Emma.

He frowned, looking down at Hen and Jimmy holding hands around him.

"Kids, lunch in the dining room," Dora said.

"Me too?" asked Jimmy, gripping Henrietta's hand tightly.

"Of course," said Emma.

They broke hands to let Jeremy out. As he moved away from them, they immediately joined hands again and followed them into the dining room.

Lottie walked over to Hen. "Up."

She turned to Jimmy. "Will you help get the napkins and plates out of the sideboard?" she asked as she lifted Lottie and put her into her chair.

Dora and Tim came through the kitchen door with a tray of meat, cheeses, and bread. Jeremy and Emma brought in the pitchers and glasses. Everyone sat, put together their sandwiches, and ate.

"Thanks," said Jimmy. "That was good." He sat back in his chair.

"Do you still want to see the room at the boarding house?" Dora asked him slowly, putting down her napkin.

"Can we go now?" he asked, standing quickly.

"He has to get back to work soon," Hen explained.

"I've been assigned kitchen duty today," Tim said. "I'll take care of clearing the table."

"We can help move things into the kitchen for you," Emma told him. Jeremy nodded. Patrick had already taken his plate away.

Tim followed Dora, Jimmy, and Hen to the foyer. "Wait, the doctor said you need to stay out of the cold," he told Dora.

"The wind's down today," Hen said.

"You're not up to Dick?" Jimmy asked Dora.

"Not up to what?" she asked.

"He asked if you're not feeling well," Emma explained.

"I'm fine," Dora told him. "Just a little under the weather is all." She turned to Tim. "I'll bundle up," she promised, "and I'll go straight in."

He relented and got her coat. He wrapped her scarf tightly around her face. She mumbled something. He lowered the scarf. "Yes?"

"Can't breathe," she wheezed.

"Good, that means you're wrapped up," he said as he folded the scarf back and pulled on her hat. He pointed at Hen and Jimmy. "Make sure she's outside for a limited time."

"We will, I promise," Hen reassured him.

The three exited and Tim stood at the door watching them make their way over to the next house. Once they were inside, he nodded and went back to work.

Dora opened the door of the boarding house, and they entered. She started to unwrap when Mark and Enzo ran by them.

"Boys," Dora called after them when she unwrapped her scarf, "coats, please."

Enzo shook his head. "Someone's always telling me to wear a coat," he grumbled. Mark just grinned and tossed it to his friend. They put them on and headed out the door.

"Mrs. Spencer!" Dora called out.

A woman with dark gray-streaked hair walked out of the dining room. "Well, hello, Dora. Is there something I can help with?"

"No, I'm just showing the empty rooms to a potential new boarder. Jimmy MacDonald, this is Mrs. Spencer. She runs things over here."

"Well, I try," the woman said dryly. "Go on up, the rooms are cleaned and ready."

"Nice to meet you," Jimmy told her.

"You too," she said and walked back into the dining room.

The three walked upstairs, and Dora pushed open the door of the smaller room. Jimmy entered quickly and saw a nicely sized room with a bed, a dresser, and a desk. There was also a large fireplace on the opposite wall. "Lally-cooler," he said approvingly.

"Lally-cooler. You used that expression before to describe us. What does it mean?" Dora asked him.

"A nice thing, a real success. I just meant it's perfect."

Dora smiled. "I like that."

"When can I move in?"

She told him the amount and said firmly, "Jimmy, the rent will be due before you move in."

"I can pay weekly," he said. "Do I get breakfast and dinner?"

"You do. It also includes a bag lunch for you to take with you to work."

Hen's eyes widened. Lunch was always an extra. Jimmy turned away from them to look at the room again. Dora held up her fingers to her lips to stop her from commenting. She nodded.

Jimmy turned back to them, held out his hand, and said, "It's a deal."

Dora shook the offered hand. "Welcome. You can move in today if you'd like."

He pulled out his wallet and gave her a pile of money.

"This is too much," she objected.

"Just put it on the account. I don't want to end up homeless again."

She gripped the money. "If that happens, we have a temp agency that'll keep you employed."

"Really? That's great," he said with a grin.

"Like I said," Hen commented, "they're good people."

Jimmy walked to the bed and sat down. He bounced on it some to test the softness.

Dora asked, "Jimmy, what's your boss like?"

"Kind of dark," he said.

"Dark?"

"In mood and looks."

"Black eyes and dark hair?" she asked, picturing the man outside who'd been strangling the woman, the man pushing a pillow down onto her face.

"Yes."

"What does he do?"

"He's a doctor."

"I'd heard that. Does he see patients?"

"Well… sort of."

Dora clenched her hands. "What do you mean?"

"People come in and leave with bottles. They're only there a short time."

"That's odd," she mused. "Doctor's appointments should take longer. Are you ever in the room with them?"

"Nah, I'm a general handyman—building shelves, moving things around, cleaning up the house." He stood and walked around the room.

"Doesn't he have a housekeeper?"

"No, just a cook, and she doesn't leave the kitchen."

"Does he have a wife?"

He walked to the closet and opened it. "Yeah, she was gone for a little while, but she's back now." Dora thought about that. "It's odd, though," he continued.

"What is?" Hen asked.

"Before she left, she was friendly. She'd help me with various chores or just want to talk. I think she was lonely. She said I could call her Susan. She was a basket of oranges, you know?"

"Basket of oranges?" Dora asked.

"She was pretty."

"How is she now?"

"She's standoffish. I tried to ask her about a few things, and she told me I should be working, not talking. I called her Susan, and she told me I had to call her *Mrs. Smythe*."

"That's odd."

"More than that," he said in a lowered voice, "she'd been planning to leave him. She said the house and the area were just not what she wanted."

"Do you know where she was from?" Dora asked.

"Maine. She'd grown up there. She asked me to buy her a train ticket so she could get back home."

"Hmm, do you think she has family who're still there?"

"Damfino. She was gone before I could ask."

"You mentioned she'd been gone. When did she leave?"

"I don't know exactly. One day, she just wasn't there. When I asked Dr. Smythe, he said I needed to go back to work."

"Do you know when this was?" Dora asked.

"Yeah, it was two nights ago."

"That's when you were sick!" Hen said to Dora.

"Yes, it was." Another clue. "When did she return home?"

"Just yesterday."

"I think we have enough now."

Hen caught where Dora was going; she'd been at home when Dora had screamed from the kitchen. "You suspect the doctor killed his wife," she whispered.

Jimmy's jaw dropped. "Killed his wife? But… but… she's here again."

"I don't understand all of the clues," Dora admitted, "but I'm sure there's a case here. It's time to bring in the professionals."

"Professionals?" Jimmy asked.

"Emma and Jeremy, they're with the Pinkertons," Hen explained.

He whistled in surprise. "They're mutton shunters? That's some pumpkins."

"Some pumpkins," repeated Dora.

He checked his watch. "I have to get back to work." He hesitated. "Do you really think Dr. Smythe's a murderer?"

"I don't know." Dora took his hands. "Don't say anything. We need to plan. Do you understand? This is very important."

"I do." He nodded his head emphatically, then checked the time. "I have to run." He left, and his feet pounded down the stairs.

"When are you going to move in?" Hen called after him.

"Tonight!" he yelled without stopping.

"Come over after dinner for the tree trimming!" Dora added.

"I'll be there!" The door slammed behind him.

"Will he be safe over there?" Hen asked, wringing her hands.

"He seems like an intelligent young man; I think he'll be careful."

"What'll we do next?"

"Bring the team in."

"When?"

"I think after the tree trimming."

CHAPTER 14

The afternoon flew by. Tim got Dora to lie down, and then joined the rest to clean the house.

Dora slept hard; she wanted to be ready for the presentation of the case to the team.

"Dora! Dora!"

"What? What is it? Tim, is that you?" she called through the fog. "Tim, I can't find you."

She heard him calling, and she started to run toward the voice. "Dora! Dora!" She saw a large figure and ran over to him. "Tim, I'm here."

The figure turned, and it wasn't Tim! It was the man with the dark eyes. His hands reached for her.

She sat up in bed, screaming, clutching her throat.

The door crashed open, and three out-of-breath people ran into the room.

"Is someone in here?" Emma demanded, running to the window, her knife in her hand.

Tim rushed over to Dora. "What happened?"

Jeremy looked around. "I don't see anything."

Dora was holding her hand to her chest, gasping for breath. "It was a dream. A scary dream, but just a dream."

Emma slid her knife back in its sheath and walked over to kiss her on the head. "You scared the hell out of us."

"I didn't mean to."

"I know." She turned to Jeremy. "Let's give them some space."

Tim sat down. "Did you get any rest?" he asked.

"I did," she assured him. "It was just a bad dream."

"Do you want to stay in bed longer?"

She groaned. "The last thing I want to do is go back to sleep."

"Great, we could use some help setting up for tonight."

She looked at the clock. "Have I missed dinner?"

"No, it's ready. Emma helped me, and Ethyl got back in time to assist."

"I'll get dressed."

"Need some help?"

"No, I think I'll be okay."

"Want me to wait for you?"

"No, go on down. I'll be right behind you."

He left, and she let out the breath she was holding. *It has to be tonight. They have to believe me.*

She dressed quickly and pulled her hair into a loose bun. On the way down, she passed Tim carrying boxes down the stairs. "Is that all the decorations?"

"I have one more trip to make, and that should be all of them."

They heard the dinner bell ring. "You can get it after," she told him. "Let's go eat now. I can't wait to see what we're having." She walked into the dining room and burst out laughing. It was breakfast for dinner.

"It seemed that the only things I could make were for breakfast." He smiled. "Is it okay?"

"It looks amazing," she said, smiling back at him.

Everyone sat down to enjoy pancakes, waffles, sausages,

bacon, biscuits, and eggs. As they were cleaning up, Lottie ran into the kitchen.

"The tree! The tree! It's time to decorate the tree!" she chanted.

"The best night of the year," agreed Dora.

"Now that you're on the mend, I agree," said Tim. He leaned down to kiss her.

"Oh, yuck," Jeremy said, entering the kitchen. "She needs her rest." Tim and Dora giggled and stuck their tongues out at him. He grinned and put his plate on the counter.

Henrietta ran in and picked up Lottie, swinging her around until the little girl giggled. "Can we help with the cookies?" she asked.

"Of course. The boxes are over there," Dora pointed out. Hen and Lottie went to retrieve them. She took the boxes and handed one to Lottie. Tim got down the trays and laid them on the table.

Ethyl stood at the stove. They could hear a popping noise. "I see that Ethyl has the popcorn started," Dora said. Emma carried in the pitchers used at dinner. "Can you make the punch, sister?" Dora asked her.

"I can." Emma got out two punch bowls: one for rum punch for the adults and fruit punch for the kids.

"We'll need to keep them separate," Dora reminded her.

"I will."

They heard a knock on the front door. "Want me to get it?" asked Patrick from the doorway.

"Were we expecting someone?" Tim asked.

"Yes," said Dora. "I invited Jimmy."

Both men rolled their eyes at her. "We're going to need a translator," Jeremy muttered.

"Don't look at me," Patrick told them. "You can figure that out on your own."

"I'll let him in," Emma said. She went and opened the door.

Jimmy was smoothing his hair. When he saw her, he put his hands down quickly.

"I was invited," he said nervously.

"I know, welcome. We're getting organized."

"Can I help?"

"Follow me."

They entered the kitchen, and Dora called, "Did you get to eat at the boarding house?"

"I did; Mrs. Spencer's a great cook for someone dizzy age."

"She is." *I think that was the right answer*, thought Dora.

Emma asked, "Have you already moved in?"

"I didn't have much to move, so it was easy."

Emma thought about that. Christmas was coming, and they might be able to fix that. She whispered in Jeremy's ear. "Sure, we can do that," he responded.

"Tomorrow?"

He nodded.

The trays of cookies were ready. Jimmy carried one and Hen the other. Ethyl followed with the popcorn, and Emma with the two containers of punch. Jeremy joined them with a cake and a pie.

"We forgot the—" Dora started.

"Cranberries?" asked Patrick.

"They're in the kitchen," said Dora.

"I'll get them," he said. He returned and sat down to start stringing the popcorn and cranberries.

"I wanna help," Lottie said.

"Here, sit here next to me," he told her. "Do one popcorn and then one cranberry."

Snacks were passed out, and the punch was poured.

"Can I have some punch from that one?" Jimmy asked, pointing at the adult punch.

"This one?" Emma asked. She poured a cup and took a long

drink. "Nope," she said with a grin. "You can have the other one."

"Aw, that one's for kids," he complained.

"You're still a kid," teased Hen. "You don't want to be arf'ar-f'an'arf." He took the cup from her good naturedly and grimaced at the fruit punch as he drank.

Tim and Jeremy got up and opened the boxes around the tree. Hen pulled Jimmy to the tree to help. Tim looked at Patrick. "Help me with the angel?" he asked his son.

"Sure." Tim bent down, and Patrick climbed up on his shoulders. Dora handed the angel to him, and he placed it atop the tree. When it was placed per Dora's instructions, Tim kneeled so Patrick could climb off his shoulders and return to the popcorn and cranberry stringing with Lottie.

The tree came together, and the family sat looking at it. "Too bad Abbey, Cole, and Papa couldn't be here," Dora commented sadly.

"We're a little off schedule, and they had prior commitments," Tim said. "We'll see them at the Christmas party."

"Mama?" Lottie asked as she sat cuddled up between Dora and Tim.

"Yes, dear?"

"When will we have presents?"

The group laughed. Dora answered, "I might wrap some tonight, Lottie." She grinned and laid her head on Dora's lap. Within a few moments, she was asleep.

The group looked to be breaking up and Dora spoke. "I need you all to stay."

"Is something wrong?" Emma asked her.

Hen, Jimmy, and Dora shared a look. Dora answered slowly. "Maybe. We need your help to review something."

"We?" asked Emma.

"Me, Hen, and Jimmy."

"Can everyone stay?" Tim asked her, looking down at a sleeping Lottie.

"Yes, I think so. She should sleep through the discussion."

"Go on, tell us," Jeremy encouraged her.

"At first, I know you thought what I saw when I was sick was a hallucination." They nodded. "Dr. Phillips told me that the medicine I was given by Dr. Smythe was a high dose of opium and that might have caused my initial problems. Since I've stopped taking it, my thoughts have been clearer, and my memory's coming back."

"What do Hen and Jimmy have to do with this?" Emma asked.

"I confirmed some odd things going on over at the doctor's house," Jimmy commented.

Tim said, "Like what?"

"His wife, Susan. She'd disappeared for a few days after Dora saw her outside."

"When I saw Dr. Smythe, or someone who looked like him, strangle the woman next door," Dora explained.

"But she's back now?" asked Emma.

"Maybe," he faltered. "She's both the same and different."

"How is that?" she asked.

"Before Susan disappeared, she'd been planning to go back home to get away from him."

"How did you know her plans?" asked Jeremy.

"We were friends; we talked when Dr. Smythe wasn't around. I think she was lonely."

"Did he know?" Emma asked.

"We didn't think so."

"Is there anything else?"

"Tams."

"Whose that?" asked Jeremy.

"Her dog," said Jimmy.

"The red one?" Patrick asked.

"Yeah, she's a golden retriever. How did you know about her?"

"I've seen you walking her."

"That's her dog; she raised her from a puppy. They were inseparable, and now the dog doesn't like her. She runs away and hides when Susan—sorry, *Mrs. Smythe*—enters the room."

"Dogs can sense things," Emma murmured thoughtfully.

"Is this enough to suspect the man," Tim asked, "especially if his wife appears to still be with him?"

Dora reached over and took his hand. "Was I ever left alone with him?"

Tim shook his head, and Emma corrected him. "No, we did leave for a moment; he sent me to get more blankets and you for water."

"That's right. Why?" he asked with a frown.

"Because he tried to smother me with a pillow. When that didn't work, he gave me the bottle of opium that was making me sicker and more confused."

"And we'd be less likely to believe you if you shared your theories with us." Emma groaned and said, "And I thought we were the detectives."

Tim's fists were clenched. Jeremy saw and put a hand on his arm. "We can't rush over. We need proof first."

"I brought a murderer into our home," Tim growled.

"You didn't know," Dora told him.

"I shouldn't have left you alone."

"We're both at fault. I shouldn't have trusted him blindly," Emma admitted.

"You both are listening to me now," said Dora.

"We are," she and Tim confirmed.

"Another murder," Emma murmured.

"Well, it is Christmas, and I've come to expect murder during this time of year," Jeremy said.

"Is this normal for your family?" Jimmy whispered to Hen.

"It has been," she said. "Last year, it was a serial killer."

"That was you guys?" he asked. "I read about that. That was mad as hops. It was based on the song, right?"

"The Twelve Days of Christmas," Emma confirmed.

"And before that?"

"A party with murders, and before that was a haunted house," Emma said, ticking off her list.

"Some pumpkins," Dora said.

"What does that mean?" Tim asked her.

"She means wow," Henrietta told him.

Tim looked between Dora and Jimmy.

"What do we do next?" Dora asked the group.

Emma sat forward. "I have an idea and, Jimmy, I think you can help with it." She discussed her plan.

"There won't be danger for Jimmy and Hen?" asked Dora.

"Not if we keep our part of the bargain."

CHAPTER 15

The next day, Emma and Jeremy headed out early to start their plan. "Tell Jimmy we'll have it for him at lunch time," Emma told Hen.

"I'll go over to the boarding house and tell him before he goes to work," she said.

"Are you working at the bakery today?"

"I'm off. I told them I'd work tomorrow morning."

"Good," Jeremy said, "enjoy your holidays."

"And catch a murderer," she reminded him with a grin.

"Well, you are part of the family. It's what we do during the holidays."

She grinned. "I'll be right back."

She got to the door, and Dora called out, "Coat!"

"But I'm just going next..." Dora only stared. "I'll get my coat," Henrietta grumbled. She pulled it on. "Okay now?"

Dora nodded and waved to her. "Get going."

Hen hurried out. It wasn't long before she came back out of breath. "He'll come over for lunch."

"Good," said Emma. "Ready to go?" she asked Jeremy.

"Ready when you are."

"We're on our way," Emma said.

"See you at lunch," Dora replied and walked to the dining room.

"Lottie, want to come to my room to play?" Hen asked the girl.

"Yes, please."

"Carry or walk?" She held up her arms. "Carry, it is." She lifted her up and they went up the stairs to her room.

"We seem to be feeding that boy a lot," said Tim.

"He's helping us out," Dora reminded him.

"I guess..."

"And he needs someone; he's all alone."

"You're right, we need to help."

They had a slow morning. Tim worked on his books, and Ethyl filled the house with the smell of baking cookies and bread.

"Should I set the table?" Ethyl asked from the doorway of the sitting room.

"Is it lunch time already?" Dora asked.

"It is."

"We're expecting Emma, Jeremy, and Jimmy. Let's give them a few more minutes."

The minutes passed. They heard knocking on the door. "Jimmy's here," said Dora.

"I'll get it," Tim told her. He stood, went to the door, and opened it. Jimmy stood there, his face red and wet with tears.

"Jimmy, are you okay?" Tim asked and pulled him into the house. "Did something happen to you?"

"He killed Tams, Susan's dog!" he cried, putting his face in his hands.

Dora rushed out. "Bring him in here. Ethyl, get a wet cloth," she said.

Tim walked Jimmy over to the settee and sat him down. He went to the foyer and called out, "Hen!"

She and Lottie started down the stairs. She saw Tim's frown. "What happened?"

"Jimmy's here and he's upset. It seems that Dr. Smythe killed his wife's dog."

"Oh, no! Is he all right?"

He met her at the base of the stairs and took Lottie. "Why don't you go in and talk to him. Go on," he encouraged when she hesitated. He looked down at Lottie. "How would you like to see Ethyl?" She nodded, and he walked her to the dining room.

Ethyl met him and handed him the wet rag. She took Lottie's hand and said, "I have something for you to taste in the kitchen."

Tim carried the rag to Jimmy. "Put this on your neck. And breathe." Jimmy did as he directed. "Now, tell us what happened."

"Tams was scratching on the basement door. She'd been doing that since Susan went away. I know it bothered Dr. Smythe, but I'd pull her away and distract her. I'm not there all the time, and she damaged the door."

"Why do you think she's dead?" Dora asked.

"She just disappeared, and when I asked, Dr. Smythe said she was taken care of and it wasn't any of my business."

"I'm not sure we should go through with our plan," Dora said.

Jeremy, Emma, and Patrick walked in at that time. They took off their coats, set their boxes down, and found the morose people in the sitting room. "What's wrong?" Emma asked.

"Dr. Smythe may have killed Tams," Hen told her.

"The dog?"

"Yes."

Emma and Jeremy looked at each other. "All right," Emma said. "We need to regroup. First off, Jimmy and Henrietta shouldn't be involved anymore."

"I agree," said Dora. "This is too much."

Jimmy took the rag off his neck and said, "I'm going back, whether you support me or not."

Hen reached out to him. "I'm with you."

"Let's all take a breath," Jeremy cautioned them. "We'll be watching Dr. Smythe and his wife at the party. Jimmy and Hen won't be at risk in the house."

Dora stared at him. "Okay, I'd rather we operated as a team. I'll be here, watching them."

"Don't forget about me," Patrick spoke up. "I can help."

"It's time Dr. Smythe is held accountable," Jimmy spat out. "He needs to be Chicagoed!"

"That he does," Emma agreed. "We're moving forward?" she asked the group. At everyone's nod, she reached into her skirt pocket and handed Jimmy an invitation to the Charity Gala that evening. She and Jeremy had gone to see Clair that morning to get the invitation. "Do you think they'll attend?" she asked him.

"Yeah, 'Susan's' been complaining about not getting any invitations to social events." He turned the envelope over. "She'll be all enthuzimuzzy over this." He started to head out.

"Jimmy, can you stay to eat?" Dora asked him.

He turned back to them. "No, I'm good."

"Wait a moment." She ran to the kitchen and brought back a sack; she'd put some cookies and an apple in it. "Take this. It may help you get your appetite back."

He took it and sucked in a deep breath. "I'll be here after dinner this evening."

"I'll walk you to the door," Hen said. She closed the door behind him and walked back to the room. "Will he be okay?"

"I hope so," Dora replied.

They moved into lunch, though they mostly just picked at their food. The afternoon went by quickly, and after dinner Emma asked Dora, "Can you help me with my dress?"

"Of course," she said, looking at Tim. "Can you go check on Jimmy?"

He nodded and stood. Hen asked him, "Can I come?"

"Sure, grab your coat."

"Lottie, would you like to see Aunt Emma getting ready?" Emma asked the little girl.

"Oh, yes!" she squealed happily and started to run toward Emma. Dora held her back and said, "I think we need to make sure you aren't sticky first."

"Okay, Mama."

"Let me get her washed up, and we'll meet you upstairs," Dora told Emma.

Emma said, "I'll see you up there."

She started up the stairs, then stopped at Dora's voice. "I don't like the plans for tonight."

"Hey—this will be fine. We'll keep them safe."

"I know, I just wish the kids could be kept out of it."

"When I was sixteen, what was I doing at that time?"

"Getting into as much trouble as you could," she admitted.

"And catching the bad guys?"

"Yes."

"So, we let them do the same, but we're the backup."

She nodded and Emma went up to the sewing room and walked over to the long dress on the form.

"It's a beautiful dress," Dora said from the door. Lottie was in her arms.

"Down," Lottie demanded.

"Only if you stay over by the beds and don't touch the dress. Can you do that?" Dora asked.

Lottie tilted her head. "Okay, Mama."

Emma walked around the dress. "It's lovely. I wish you could be there with us."

"Me too, but I will be here watching the house." She looked out the window facing the doctor's house. "What if Dr. and Mrs. Smythe don't go tonight?"

"Then Jimmy might do something on his own, without our protection."

"We don't want that. Now, sit. I need to work on your hair."

Emma sat and Lottie demanded, "Me next, me next!"

"After we get Emma dressed and off to the party," Dora promised her. She brushed Emma's hair and started to braid different sections. "Lottie, bring me that headpiece there on the bed."

She picked up the pear headpiece and walked it over. Dora took it and placed it on Emma's head and continued to work the braids around it.

Emma turned in the mirror. "It's lovely, thank you."

"It looks just like a crown, Mama," Lottie gushed.

"It does, doesn't it," Dora agreed. "Want some makeup?" she asked Emma.

"Yes, please. Some rouge on my cheeks and lips." After the makeup was applied, Dora stood back.

"Time for the dress." Dora took the dress off the form and set it on the ground. The deep blue velvet pooled on the floor. Emma stepped into the center and pulled it up. The sleeves were full and puffed, and the bodice was cut low and had a dropped waistline. Butterfly arrangements on the bodice sparkled in the light.

"The velvet's so elegant," commented Dora, walking around her and checking the hem.

"And heavy," Emma replied.

Dora fluffed up the lighter fabric around her neck, filling in some of the low neckline. She blotted her eyes with her handkerchief. "You look lovely."

"Oh, Dora, don't make me cry. Help me take this off, and I'll stay home with you. The boys can manage things at the event."

She sniffed. "No, you're going. I worked too hard on this look to have you stay home. Come on, let's go downstairs."

Emma laughed. "I need help with my shoes."

"I guess you'll need those."

Emma sat on the stool and Dora put on her shoes. "There, now stand."

"You look like a queen," Hen said from the door.

"You know, she kind of does," Dora said. They walked down together.

"Remember, walk slow," Hen murmured. "You want to make an entrance."

Emma took her hand and smiled. "I'll do that."

The three women went downstairs, and the men were in their black suits waiting. Jeremy whistled at Emma. She blushed and continued down the stairs. "You look beautiful. But you're missing something," he said.

"Am I?" she asked, touching her hair.

He snapped his fingers. "I think I know what it is," He reached into his pocket and pulled out a long box. Dora and Hen stepped closer. Jeremy opened the box and revealed a necklace with a ruby surrounded by diamonds. Two gold chains went around the neck, and two hung from the base, with rubies at the ends.

Emma put a hand to her mouth. "Turn," he requested. She turned and waited. She could feel it going around her neck. She reached up and touched it.

"Oh, Jeremy, I love it," she bubbled.

"I've had it for you for a while."

"Thank you."

Dora elbowed Tim in the stomach. "Ow! What?" He glanced at Dora and got the silent message. "Oh, uh, you look nice."

"Thanks, Tim."

"Hen, Jimmy is in the sitting room," said Tim.

She nodded and went to join him. The group followed.

"What part do I play in all this?" Patrick asked. "Can I go with Jimmy and Hen?"

"No, you stay with Mama," Tim told him. "We need someone here to help protect her."

"Stay with me," Dora appealed. "We can watch with Emma's spyglass."

"Okay," Patrick told her.

"Jimmy, are the Smythe's going to the event?" Emma asked.

Mrs. Smythe's mad as hops; she was running around saying she didn't have anything to wear on such short notice."

"But they are going," she pressed.

"They sent me with the RSVP. They'll be there."

"You watch for them to leave before you enter the house," directed Jeremy.

"Where will you go first, Jimmy?" Dora asked him.

"The basement. I think Tams knew something was down there."

"Do it quickly and get out," Emma said. "We don't want to push the time."

"Got it."

Patrick asked, "Aunt Emma, where's your spyglass?"

"My room, right-hand drawer." He ran up the stairs.

"What about your torch?" Dora asked her.

"That's a good idea." She walked over to the staircase and called up. "Patrick, get my torch from my bedside."

"I will." He came back down the stairs quickly and handed the two items to Emma.

She held up the torch and showed Jimmy and Hen how to use it. "It's limited in use but should work just fine inside the house. Don't turn on any other lights," Emma cautioned. "Wave at Dora and Patrick so that they know when you enter and when you leave."

"I will," he acknowledged.

Emma was frowning. Hen went over to her. "You're spoiling your look." She reached up and smoothed out her frown. "No worries. We'll be in and out."

Emma pulled her close. "I love you so much; be safe."

"I love you, too. Don't you three have a party to get to?"

They heard knocking at the door. "That should be the carriage now," Tim said.

Jeremy got out Emma's long dark coat and a dark scarf to cover her hair.

"Lightly, watch your hair," cautioned Dora.

They were ready and went out the front door and down the steps. The three climbed into the carriage. Patrick said, "There they go."

"Yes." Dora waved at them.

"No, the people next door."

"What?" She looked to the right and saw Dr. and Mrs. Smythe getting into a cab. "The game's afoot. Let's move inside." She and Patrick did so and closed the door.

Jimmy and Hen had changed into dark clothes and were standing in the dining room. Patrick and Dora joined them. "Listen, you two, just get in and try that door."

"We will," they said together.

"Go out the kitchen door and stay low."

CHAPTER 16

The carriage approached the entrance of the mansion where the gala was taking place. The line started and stopped as the carriages in front of them were unloaded. When it was their turn, Tim got out, and Jeremy followed. He turned back to help Emma out. Tim led the way, and Emma and Jeremy followed up the stone staircase into the building.

"Are they behind us?" she murmured.

Jeremy glanced behind him. "Yeah, they're here. The only part of this I don't get is, if his wife's dead, how come we have a duplicate here?"

"That's the question. Is she the same woman?"

"Jimmy says yes and no."

They got inside the decorated mansion; garland was draped on all surfaces, and red ribbon wound its way through it. Emma looked up. It was even hung on the crystal chandeliers.

"Has Clair arrived?" Emma asked the butler standing at the door.

"Yes, madam, she's in the long hall."

"Thank you," she replied. They stopped and looked around. "Festive tonight," she said. Tim and Jeremy agreed.

Another butler came up and helped her remove her coat. Tim and Jeremy handed theirs to him, as well. They heard the couple behind them announce themselves as Dr. Robert and Mrs. Susan Smythe. After they walked away, they could hear the couple arguing.

"I don't know why we're here," Smythe groused.

"It's a social event; you know that word?" taunted Susan.

"Just shut up."

"You can't tell me what to do."

"I can tell you the dress you're wearing shows too much."

"Too much what?" Susan asked. Her tone had an edge to it.

"Never mind."

"They are not getting along," Jeremy mused.

"Let's move further in," Tim said.

They knew the assignment; watch them and keep them there while Hen and Jimmy were inside their house.

CHAPTER 17

*H*en and Jimmy exited the kitchen door and made their way through the side yard. They were in lighter coats to be able to get in and out quicker. Jimmy guided her to the fence. He'd moved a ladder there earlier. He propped it up on the fence and started up. Once at the top, he jumped down, and she followed behind him. When she came to the top, he lifted his arms. She leaped and he caught her. Setting her down on her feet, they made their way to the back door.

"How do we get in?" she whispered.

"I have a key," he said, pulling it out of his pocket. "The other Susan gave it to me when she wanted me to get her out."

She nodded as he unlocked the door. They slowly entered the dark kitchen.

"Light the lantern and flash it at the window," she reminded him.

He lit it and swung it in the window, then extinguished it quickly.

CHAPTER 18

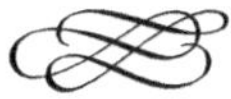

$\mathcal{P}$atrick pointed to the house. "I see the light."

Dora moved the spyglass in the direction he mentioned. "I see it. Good, they lowered it immediately."

"What do we do now?"

"I'll go to the front and keep a lookout," she told him. "We need to make sure no one goes in the front."

"I'll stay here and watch for any signal," he said as Dora moved to the front door to watch the street.

CHAPTER 19

Tim took a sip of his champagne. "I wish Dora was here. She would've loved the decorations."

"I know," Emma said, looking around. "Where are Dr. and Mrs. Smythe?"

Jeremy raised his glass toward the stairs. "She wants to mingle and he doesn't want to be here. He keeps yanking on her arm."

"I hope his patience is longer than it takes Jimmy and Hen to get in and get out," Tim said.

"I have an idea." Emma waved to Clair.

She nodded and turned back to smile easily at the man in front of her. She turned gracefully from him and waved at Thomas to join Emma, Jeremy, and Tim. Her expression stayed relaxed as she walked up. "Are they here?"

"Over there," commented Jeremy with a nod.

She glanced at the couple. "Pretty girl, though he doesn't appear to be happy to be here."

"That's where you come in," Emma told her.

Clair raised her eyebrow. "Oh, really?"

Emma grinned. "That'd give the man a heart attack."

"What're you thinking?"

CHAPTER 20

"Follow me," Jimmy told Hen, moving quickly through the house.

"What's all this stuff?" Hen asked. There were boxes lining the walls.

"Bottles."

She opened one and removed a single bottle. "Why so many?"

"Everyone who comes in leaves with one."

"Odd way to be a doctor," she said, putting it back and closing the box.

"He doesn't even have a stethoscope."

"How do you know?"

"I clean the room where he sees patients."

"Isn't that basic equipment for a doctor?"

"I thought so."

"Where's the door to the basement?" she asked.

"Down this long hall," he said, moving quickly. She followed behind him. He stopped at the door. "He hasn't asked me to repair it," he said and ran his hand down the marks Tams had made.

"Do you have the key for this one?"

"No, we might have to break it down."

She reached out and felt it. "Seems thick."

"You don't understand how angry I am." He reared back and kicked it. He kicked it over and over again.

"Maybe…" she started. The door gave enough to allow them entry. She looked at the damage he'd wreaked. "Remind me not to have you mad at me."

He leaned over and kissed her softly. "Never. Come on, let's see where this goes." He turned the torch up and descended the stairs.

"Have you been down here before?"

"No, it's always been locked up."

"It seems deeper than our basement."

"It is deep," he agreed. They finally got to the bottom step. He asked, "Can you see a gas light?" He held up the torch, and they glanced around. "There on the wall behind you." He held up the torch, and she went to turn up the gas lamp. The area was partially illuminated.

CHAPTER 21

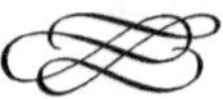

*D*ora called to Patrick, "Are they still inside?"

"I think so. I haven't seen the torch yet."

"Keep watching."

She went back to the front door and saw a wagon pulling up. "Who is that?" She squinted out the side window; it wasn't Smythe and his wife. She watched as it stopped at the house. "Oh no." She ran out and slid on the steps. She grabbed onto the handrail, pulled herself up, and stepped out into the snow. She started waving her arms and yelling at the man. "Help! Help!" she shouted, limping toward him.

He ran over to her. "What happened? Are you okay?"

"Oh no, I feel faint." She fell into him, and they both slid to the ground.

"Hey, wake up, wake up," the man said desperately underneath her. Dora kept her eyes closed and moaned. "Lady, I can't get us up by myself. Please wake up." She moaned again.

"Mama! Mama!" Patrick yelled. "Thank god you found her," he told the man.

Dora opened one eye and saw Patrick running over to them.

She sat up and glared at the man. "Why did you grab me like that?" she demanded.

"Wha? I didn't… I was… I was just trying to help," he stuttered. "You rushed up and…"

"Did he do something, Mama?" Patrick asked. "Did he hurt you? Do I need to call the police?" he asked, pulling Dora to her feet.

The man watched them helplessly from the ground. "Please don't. I don't understand what's going on," the man said, his eyes wide and his hands held out in front of him. "I was just trying to help her."

"Maybe you should leave," Patrick suggested, holding onto Dora's hand, "before I call for the police."

"But… But… I'm supposed to deliver some boxes."

"You should go," Dora said, "or stay, and we'll call the authorities."

"I guess I can come back tomorrow."

He tried to stand and couldn't find purchase on the snow-encrusted grass. They watched him slip and slide. Dora nudged Patrick. He grimaced and offered the man a hand to get up. There were several attempts, and on the third try, the man's feet finally found stability.

He looked at the house, then back at them. "I'm leaving now."

"Yes, why don't you do that?"

"He won't like it," he muttered.

"Who?" Dora asked.

"Doctor Smythe."

"What's in the boxes?"

"Bottles."

"You can leave now," Patrick told him.

"I don't know how I'm going to explain this," he muttered and walked off to his wagon.

They watched him go. Dora shivered, and Patrick said, "Mama, you aren't supposed to be outside."

"Did Jimmy and Hen get out?"

"They did; I ran to get you as soon as I could."

"You know, Patrick," she said, putting her arms around his shoulders, "we make a great team."

"Yes, we do." They watched the man leave, then laughed and turned around to go back inside.

"We might want to keep this from your papa."

"What? You never left the house." Patrick grinned.

"That's my boy."

They went back into the house and saw Hen and Jimmy taking off their coats and hats.

"What'd you find?" Patrick asked.

Jeremy checked his watch. "Should we give them more time?"

"I'm not sure we have it," Tim said. "They're arguing again."

They watched Smythe tugging on his wife's arm, trying to pull her away from the group of men surrounding her.

"That necklace she's wearing looks real," Emma commented.

Abbey came up beside her and said, "It is."

"You would know, Mom," teased Jeremy and he leaned down to kiss her cheek.

"I do know my diamonds."

"As long as you don't take them," Ellis told her as he came up beside his wife.

"It is tempting, and there're plenty of distractions." The party had grown as the night went on.

"Who are we watching and why?" Ellis asked.

Emma nodded at the Smythes. "Them. Dora thinks she saw the man murder someone, and we're staking them out. Meanwhile, Hen and a friend of hers are snooping in their house, looking for clues."

"So, just another typical Christmas, eh?"

"That's what I've been saying." Jeremy chuckled.

"It looks like they're leaving," Tim said. He looked like he was going to stop them.

"No," said Emma, "I think it's time for that distraction." She waved at Clair.

She nodded toward them and headed to Smythe and his wife.

"Whew, speaking of distractions," Jeremy said, watching Clair glide across the room. She could quiet a room with her regal look. As she got nearer to the doctor and his wife, his frown changed to bemusement as he stared at her.

"Now Mrs. Smythe, or whoever she is, looks angry," Tim said.

"I knew she'd be able to delay them," Emma replied.

"Knowing Clair, she'll not only get him to stay, but she'll get a large check out of him to boot," murmured Jeremy.

"Well, the charity does well for a reason," Emma stated.

"All to a good cause," Jeremy said, holding up his glass. They clinked their glasses and continued to watch.

Emma pulled on his arm. "Look! He's writing a check."

"Tell her to cash it as soon as possible," Tim advised.

"You bet." They continued to watch Clair and the couple. "Look," she said, "now Mrs. Smythe is pulling on him, trying to get him to leave."

"Yeah, well, Clair is getting more attention than she is," Jeremy commented.

They continued to monitor the couple.

CHAPTER 23

Hen, Jimmy, Dora, and Patrick were in the sitting room. The lights were low, and the tree was lit up. Dora had made cider, and they sat enjoying the quiet.

The door opened, and they could hear laughing in the foyer. Dora stood and told the kids, "Wait here." They nodded and went back to talking in low voices. Dora waited for them to remove their coats.

Tim saw her, walked over, and kissed her. "Still up?"

"Yes, the kids are still up, too. Well, except Lottie; she went to bed earlier."

"Let's go see them."

Emma and Jeremy followed. Jeremy turned up the lights. "Ooo, is that cider?" Emma asked.

"It is," Dora responded.

Emma moved to pour herself a cup.

"Me too, please," Jeremy said.

"And me," Tim added.

Emma poured the cups, and they got settled into the room.

"Jimmy, tell us what you saw," Tim stated.

"Sure." He looked at Hen. "You can talk if you want." She nodded. "We got into the house through the back."

"He had a key," Hen volunteered.

"The other Susan gave it to me; it was part of her escape plan."

"Go on," Emma prompted. "What did you see when you got into the house?"

"Bottles," Hen said. "Boxes and boxes of bottles."

"What did they have in them?" asked Jeremy.

"They were empty."

"Why so many?" Emma asked. "What are they for?"

"I'm not sure," Jimmy admitted, "but every patient who comes in has one with them when they leave." Tim frowned and got up, leaving the room in a hurry. "Is something wrong?" Jimmy asked.

"I'm not sure," admitted Dora, listening to Tim's running steps on the stairs.

"Should I wait for him?"

"Let's take a minute," she suggested. She watched the doorway, waiting for Tim's return.

He appeared suddenly and had Dora's sketch book with him. He handed the opened book to Jimmy. "Do the bottles look like this?"

Jimmy looked at the rough sketch and said. "Yeah. How did you know??"

"Dammit," Tim growled, his hand tightening into fist. "Is he even a real doctor?"

"Jimmy doesn't think he is," Hen said.

"He doesn't even have a stethoscope or any other kind of medical equipment, and the patients are only in the room for a minute."

Tim loosened his grip, and Emma took the bottle from him. "Dr. Phillips said there was far too much opium being given to Dora," he said.

"Jeremy, I think this links to some of the cases we've seen lately," said Emma.

"What's going on?" Jimmy asked.

Jeremy looked at him. "We've been contacted by a large number of families telling us their children, husbands, and wives are taking opium. And it's taking over their lives."

"And grandparents, too," Emma added. "Most are being given more and more medication instead of monitoring their illnesses."

"He's getting them addicted," Tim surmised.

"And building in customers," Jeremy commented.

"Until they run out of money," Emma added.

"Can't they just stop like I did?" Dora asked.

"Not everyone's the same as you," Emma told her sister. "You were lucky. Some people can take it once and feel they have to have it after that."

"That'd explain why we get so many return patients," Jimmy postulated. "They come in all batty-fang and when they leave, they seem calmer and happier," he said.

Emma asked, "Is that all you saw?" Jimmy went quiet.

Hen said, "We also went to the door Tams had been scratching."

"Was it open?"

He hung his head. "It is now."

Emma looked at Jeremy and back at Jimmy. "Tell us what happened."

Hen took over. "The door was locked and Jimmy wanted to get down into the basement."

"So, I kicked it in," he said.

Dora gripped Tim's hand. "He'll know someone was in the house."

"We went down into the basement," Jimmy continued.

"It's deep," Hen added.

"What did you find once you got down there?" asked Jeremy.

"The place is set up with a lot of long hallways leading to a large metal door."

"What was inside of them?" Tim asked.

"All the doors were solid; we couldn't budge any of them."

"We need to know what's in those rooms," Emma muttered to Jeremy.

"It's time to remove Jimmy and Hen from this," he said in the same tone. "Jimmy, I think it's time you stopped working there." Dora and Tim nodded.

Hen took his hand. "I think they're right. This is too much for you."

"I want to be able to stay at the boarding house, and I can't do that without a job," he said, his eyes filling with tears.

"There might be a problem if he just disappears. Smythe might suspect something's up. Jimmy, do you think you can handle being there a little longer?" asked Emma.

He wiped his eyes. "Yes, I want to do it for Susan."

"Jimmy, if anything happens, don't wait; get out of there," Tim stressed.

"I'll do that."

Dora stood up. "Well, I think it's time for everyone to go to bed."

"Thanks for helping me," Jimmy said to the group.

"Me too," Dora said. "The last few days have been so confusing."

They stood, and Hen said, "Wait. What're the next steps?"

"We figure out a way to get me in, so we can get those basement doors opened," Emma said.

"I'm not sure you should go in there," Jimmy told her.

Emma flashed a rather evil smile. "There's no need to be worried. I do this type of thing all the time."

Jimmy looked at everyone. "I'm glad to have found you all."

"We are, too," Emma replied, and the rest nodded.

Hen walked Jimmy to the door. "Thanks for coming with me tonight," he said.

"Hey, we're friends. I'm here whenever you need me." He leaned over and kissed her on the cheek. He turned to leave. "Jimmy?" she asked softly.

"Yeah?"

"What was in the note?"

He started to deny it, but asked instead, "You saw that?"

"I did."

"I thought I was being so smooth." She waited. "I wanted to make a point. I told him I knew what he'd done."

"Dammit, Jimmy."

"What?" he asked defensively. "I didn't sign it."

"Won't he know your handwriting?"

"He thinks I'm too ignorant to write."

CHAPTER 24

At breakfast the next day Dora asked, "How're we going to get the Smythes out of the house?"

Emma smiled. "Our Christmas party."

"It makes the most sense," Tim agreed.

"But will they come?" Dora asked.

"Oh, I think we can guarantee that," murmured Emma.

"How?"

"Clair's going to be here."

"Why would that matter?"

"Let's just say the good doctor was somewhat infatuated with her at the party."

"He did write a very large check that night." Tim smiled.

"Oh, I do wish I'd seen that," Dora huffed.

"Hen, are you going into work later today?" asked Emma.

"Yeah," she said, tapping her fork on her plate.

"What's wrong?" Jeremy asked.

"Um… I need to tell you something."

"What is it?"

She sighed and looked at them. "Jimmy left a note for the doctor last night."

"Dammit," Emma swore.

"That's what I said."

"What did it say?" Jeremy asked her.

"The note said he knew that he'd killed his wife."

"Where'd he put the letter?" Emma asked, drumming her fingers on her lips.

"On the main table in the foyer."

"You think he would've already opened it?" Jeremy looked at Emma.

"We need to find out."

"How?" Dora asked.

"Oh," Emma smiled, "I'm not up to dick. I feel like I'm coming down with something."

"Something you need to see a doctor for?" Hen asked with a smile.

"Hmmm, yes, I think so. Jeremy, could you be a dear and walk me next door to see if the good doctor would mind seeing me this morning?"

He put down his napkin. "I'll walk you over now."

"Hen," Tim told her, "go stall Jimmy. We want to do this before he goes to work."

"I'll go now," she said and got up to go find Jimmy.

Emma and Jeremy got their coats and hats and headed out. It was a short walk to the house and up the stoop.

Dora looked around at the table. Tim, Lottie, and Patrick were still seated. "I guess that means we're doing the dishes."

Patrick groaned. "When I get big, I'm going to be the one investigating, and other people can do the dishes."

Tim laughed. "Come on, you're not that big yet."

Emma and Jeremy got to the neighbor's door. "Remember you're sick," he said.

"Oh, yeah." She ducked her head and coughed. Jeremy knocked, and they waited. Emma looked at Jeremy, and he shrugged. A curtain flickered.

"We've been spotted," he said.

"I'm ready."

The door swung open. The woman standing there didn't resemble the immaculately manicured woman from the night before. She pulled her robe tighter. "What do you want so early in the morning?" she demanded.

"We'd like to see the doctor," Jeremy told her.

"Well, he isn't available."

"Couldn't you check to see if he can make time for us?"

Emma coughed loudly. "Ohhhhh," she moaned.

"He won't like it," the woman muttered.

"But you'll do it anyway?"

"Yeah, I guess so. Come in." Jeremy and Emma walked into the parlor. The woman leaned forward and got a closer look at them. Her eyes widened in surprise. "Hey! You were at the party last night. You made a speech or something." She rubbed her head, seemingly confused.

"We were," Jeremy said. "We sent you the invitation after your husband helped out when my sister-in-law was sick earlier in the week."

Her eyes went wide. "Oh yes, just a minute." She ran off.

"That should get his attention," Jeremy said.

"Jeremy," Emma said in a low voice, "the note. It's on the table." He quickly walked to the table, grabbed the note, and put it in his jacket.

Dr. Smythe entered the room. "Is there something I can help with?"

"Yes, doctor," Jeremy said, turning to him. "Emma's worried she might be coming down with the flu and wanted to speak with you just in case."

Was that a frown Emma saw on his face? It was so quick, she couldn't be sure.

"Oh, all right, follow me," he directed. Jeremy looked around at the boxes lining the walls. Smythe saw his interest. "That's the problem with moving. I've had so many patients that we haven't had a chance to get organized."

So many bottles, thought Jeremy. *How many people has this man gotten addicted?*

They walked down the hallway and saw that a door had been damaged. "What happened here?" asked Jeremy.

Emma looked up. The door to the basement had been destroyed. Jimmy's emotions were showing; could he control them when he returned to work?

"Someone broke in last night," Smythe said. "My handman will have to repair it today."

They heard knocking on the door. "Just a moment, my handyman's usually here to help with this." Smythe went to the door, and a young man entered. The man looked ill; his face was white, his body thin, and he was shaking.

"Doc, I have to see you. I just can't... I just can't... Please help me."

"Of course, let me move you to the back. Just another moment," he said to Emma and Jeremy.

Jeremy shook his head. Emma's mouth compressed.

Mrs. Smythe walked over to them. "It'll be just a minute," she told them.

"No, that's okay," Emma told her, "We're going now."

"But... But, I thought you were sick."

"I'm feeling a lot better now."

"Oh, that's good," Mrs. Smythe said, following them to the door. "Will we see you soon? Another party perhaps?"

Emma smiled brightly. "As a matter of fact, we're having a Christmas party next door."

Mrs. Smythe looked across thoughtfully at their home. "Will there be important people there?"

"Oh, yes. A lot of the same ones who were at the gala last night."

The woman reached up to pat her hair. "We'll be there."

"Do you need to confirm with your husband?"

"Who?" She looked blank for a moment and then said, "Oh yes, my husband and I'll be there."

"It's tomorrow at eight pm."

They left and walked down the street. They waved to Hen and Jimmy, who were sitting on the front stoop.

"Did you get it?" she asked as she ran over to them.

"I did," Jeremy said.

"That's good."

They reached Jimmy. "We got the note," Emma told him.

"I just felt I had to say something," he said, his head hung low on his chest.

"I understand, and we'll find out what's going on," she promised.

"What do I do now?"

"You go to work and keep your head down. We need to get organized."

"Hey, we're here for you," Hen said.

"Yeah, I know. Thanks," he said and walked off toward Smythe's house.

As Henrietta stood watching him, Emma asked her, "Aren't you supposed to be getting ready for work?"

"Right, Patrick and I are working today and tomorrow."

"Do you need a cab?" Jeremy asked.

"No," she replied, "Tim's getting out this morning to deliver checks; he's going to drop us off on his way."

"Well, go on," he told her. "I'll be by to pick you up tonight."

"Hen, see me before you leave. I want to give you a list for the party," Emma said.

Hen stood up to go inside. At the door, she turned and said, "You might talk to Dora; she has a list also."

"Of course she does." Emma smiled.

"She's back in manager mode," Jeremy commented.

"She's getting back to herself," Emma agreed.

"It's a good thing."

"It's a *great* thing," she corrected, following him inside.

They heard Patrick call out, "Papa, I'll be down in a minute." When he saw Hen, he said, "Papa wants us to go soon."

"I'll be ready. I just need to change," she said, running up the stairs.

Emma pulled out her notebook and jotted down what they'd found out about the Smythes. She walked into the dining room and sat at the table. She tapped her pencil and turned to Jeremy and Dora. "What do we know?"

"We know that Dr. Smythe is drugging his 'patients,'" Jeremy said.

"Is he even a real doctor?" Dora asked them.

"It'd be impossible to figure out without knowing what school he went to," Emma told her.

Dora said, "Wouldn't his wife know something about that?"

"She should."

"Did you ask her about the party?"

"We did," Emma confirmed. "She said they'll be here."

"Well then, I'll ask her at the party," Dora said.

Tim called out, "Patrick! Hen! Hurry up, you're going to be late. Let's shake a leg." He walked into the dining room. "Any idea where Smythe might've put his other wife?"

"I'm getting more and more suspicious about that basement," mused Emma.

"Do you think he'd just keep her body?" he asked.

"You gotta think, with the frozen ground and water, there'd be nowhere to put her. He'd have to keep the body somewhere until spring," Jeremy observed.

"Ethyl," Dora called.

Ethyl walked in from the kitchen, wiping her hands on her apron. "Yes?"

"Come have a seat." She sat and Dora continued, "The Christmas party's tomorrow."

"I know. I've started on the baking."

"We'll also have boxes of cookies and pies ordered from the bakery," Dora told her. "I have a list of what we'll need for Hen to take today. And I'll have some extra servers brought in to help in the kitchen and with the guests. Oh, and once prep is done, you can attend as a guest with Jake."

"That'll be wonderful, thank you. Amy should be back in the morning."

"Yes, she and Cole will also be here."

Emma stood and began to gather her things for the day. "I need to go by and see Clair," she said.

"We can go by this morning," Jeremy said.

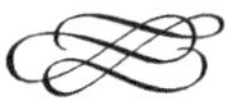

At the office, Lily, Clair's assistant, saw them walk in and said, "She's waiting for you."

"Thanks. You and Nathan going to the party?" Jeremy asked her.

"We're looking forward to it. Last night was fun, but it was work. I'm looking forward to a relaxing evening."

They walked to Clair's office and found her behind her desk. "Hello, you two." She smiled at them.

"Did you get that check in the bank?" Emma asked.

She chuckled. "I did. Thomas was waiting outside until they opened."

"Good. I don't think he'll have any spare funds soon."

"What can I do for you?"

"It's about our Christmas party," said Emma.

"Oh, we're looking forward to it."

Emma looked at Jeremy. "Go on," he said, "this was your idea."

"Yes. Tell me," Clair requested.

"We need to create a distraction to keep Dr. Smythe and his wife out of their house."

"Again?"

"Yes. We think he murdered his wife," Emma said.

"And Tams," Jeremy reminded her.

"His dog is Tams," Emma added.

Clair looked contemplative.

"If you think it's too much, we can come up with something else," said Emma.

"No, if he did kill his wife, then he deserves to be taken down. I'll play my role."

"I'm sure the missus won't appreciate it," Jeremy said.

"Yes, that's an odd relationship. We'll have to plan something for her as well," said Emma.

"Why are you so sure that this wife isn't the real wife?" Clair asked.

"There's a boy working for him, Jimmy, who's friends with Hen," Emma explained. "He said the woman's a completely different person. He's talked to both of them."

"Same looks?"

"Identical, he says," Jeremy confirmed.

"Could they be twins?" Clair suggested.

"Sisters," muttered Emma. "I should've seen that."

"You didn't stop to think that one sister would betray another like that," Jeremy said.

"No, and as we've found, not all families are close," Emma replied. "The party will be full of mischief this year."

"We need to fill Pops in on this," said Jeremy. "We might need backup to take him in. I don't think he'll go easily."

CHAPTER 26

Cole sat at his desk, reviewing their information. "That's not much to go on."

"No, that's why we need to get into the house," Emma told him.

"The basement's the answer to this," said Jeremy.

"Then we'll move forward," Cole said. "Christmas has been eventful the last few years," he added contemplatively.

"Yeah, I wouldn't mind a quiet Christmas for once," Emma agreed.

"Nah, I think you enjoy the challenge," Jeremy said.

"You're right, a quiet Christmas might be boring."

CHAPTER 27

"The party's tonight," Dora remarked, reading through her list.

"Don't do too much," Emma cautioned, rolling out cookies on the kitchen table.

"We'll all have to pitch in to get ready."

"Then I'll do extra."

"You also have me," said Ethyl from the stove.

Hen walked in through the door and watched the three busy women. She went over, put on her apron, and asked, "What can I do?"

"No, this is your vacation," Emma said. "You've been working at the bakery since the holiday started. Go enjoy your time."

Hen crossed her arms. "No, you need the help, and I'm staying."

"Can't argue with that," Jeremy said from behind her. "Let her," he mouthed at Emma.

Emma got the message. Henrietta wanted to be included in all family activities. "Well, why are you just standing there? There's work to be done."

Henrietta grinned. "How about a spice cake?" she asked.

"Sure, why don't you get it started," Emma said. The four ladies all got back to work.

Jeremy walked back to the dining room to help Tim set the table. He tossed a white tablecloth to Jeremy, who grabbed the other end and secured it.

"Candlesticks?" Tim asked.

"Got 'em." Jeremy took them from the sideboard.

"Can I help?" Lottie asked, running in.

"Sure," Tim told her, "take these and put them on the table." He handed her a stack of cloth napkins. She ran over to the table and put them in a loose pile. Tim moved a stack of plates and glasses to the table. Jeremy got out the candles and put them in the holders.

"What's missing?" Tim asked, stepping back.

"Flowers!" shouted Lottie.

"I think we can help with that," Abbey said as she entered the room.

"Mom, I didn't hear you come in," Jeremy said, walking over to kiss her on the cheek.

"We wanted to arrive before the snow gets worse."

"It's not the snow I'm worried about," Ellis said. He walked in carrying several bouquets.

Dora walked out of the kitchen, wiping her hands on her apron. "Oh, Abbey, those are perfect."

"Hey, I carried them," Ellis told her.

"Thank you, Papa," she said, walking over to kiss him on the cheek.

"How're you feeling?" he asked.

"I'm better."

"She needs to rest more," Tim pointed out.

Ellis took his daughter by the chin. "You need to take care of yourself. There are plenty of people to help."

"I know, Papa." Dora kissed Abbey on the cheek and moved

to pull out the vases for the flowers. Tim rolled his eyes at Ellis and walked over to her. He took the heavy vases. "Where do you want them?"

Her face red, she said, "At either end of the table."

"I'll bring a pitcher of water," Abbey said as she walked to the kitchen.

With everyone helping, the evening came around, and the house sparkled with candles and decorations. Dora was feeling better and had started to add decorations to every room downstairs.

"You need to slow down some," Tim said to her.

"I feel fine," she said, moving the glasses around on the table.

"Yes, but we all need to be at the top of our form tonight."

"Tim, I just don't want to be left with that man at any time."

"You won't be," he promised.

She laid her head on his chest. Lottie ran in and wrapped her arms around their legs. Tim picked her up.

"Mama, Christmas is all over the house," Lottie chirped. "And there are presents with my name on them under the tree."

"Yes, there are."

"Will there be more?"

"Maybe," Dora said. "Santa hasn't come yet."

"Santa," Lottie murmured happily.

"What're you going to wear to the party?" she asked Lottie.

"I want to wear a dress."

"I think we can work that out."

"I want a dress like Aunt Emma's."

"Well, I don't think so, but I think there's something nice we can find."

"Will it have lace?"

"Why don't we go check?"

"Okay, Mama." Dora took Lottie's hand, and they walked up the stairs.

Tim called out, "Ethyl?" She stepped out of the kitchen. "Did Jake get the picture for me?"

She nodded. "He says it'll be ready tonight."

"Good, I'll have time to frame it. Did Jake get all of his pictures completed for the show at the gallery?"

"He did; it was a busy day."

"When's the show?"

"It should be after the new year. It's a special show for local artists."

"We can't wait to see it."

"Me too."

"What'd you get Jake for Christmas?" he asked.

"He wanted a new camera."

"Those can be expensive; do you need some help with the cost?"

"I've been saving up all year," she assured him.

"Then I think this might come in handy." He walked to his books, pulled out an envelope, and handed it to her.

She opened it, and her eyes went wide. She looked up at him. "Why's it so much?"

"You got a bonus this year, and you've been covering for Amy. We wanted to reward you."

"Thank you," she said, holding it to her chest. "This is wonderful."

Tim smiled as he went over to gather the rest of the checks. His temp agency had been successful, and the bonuses would help the workers who had limited work in the winter. He stepped into the foyer and called out, "I'm leaving now if you want to do some last-minute Christmas shopping."

Henrietta and Patrick came down the stairs. "Coats and hats," he reminded them.

Hen asked, "Would it be okay if I checked on Jimmy first?"

"I think it'd be best to leave him alone for now. He's dealing with a lot."

"Tim, will you be able to get him work when this is over?"

"I have some open positions. I'll see where his interests lie."

"He's good with his hands and carpentry. He's also pretty smart."

"Hmm, there might be other options for him."

"Thanks, Tim," she said and kissed him on the cheek.

"Can we go now?" asked Patrick.

"Yes. Everybody out. We'll get the wagon and be on our way."

CHAPTER 28

"Jimmy," Dr. Smythe called.

Jimmy left the shelves he was working on and joined the doctor in the hallway. "Yes, sir?"

"Can you repair the basement door?"

"Yes, I'll need to get some wood."

Smythe took out some money. "Go down and get it today," he said. "I like things secure."

"I will."

Smythe stayed where he was. "Jimmy, have you seen anyone around the house who shouldn't be here?" he asked.

"No, sir, there wasn't anyone around when I left yesterday."

Smythe nodded. "Well, get going. I want this door repaired as soon as possible."

"Robert, we have a party to attend tonight," Susan said gaily.

"No, I already took you to one just yesterday. There'll be no more."

"This one's next door; you won't have to go far."

He frowned. "Next door?"

"Yes."

He thought about that. "Yes, I think we're going."

"Good, because I have several dresses being delivered today."

"Dresses? With whose money?"

"Why, yours, of course."

Jimmy scuffed his feet and Smythe whirled around to face him. "Why are you still here?" he demanded.

"On my way now," Jimmy squeaked and hurried off.

Smythe turned back to the woman. "As for you..." He raised his hand.

"What, are you going to hit me?" she demanded, lifting her chin.

He swung, and she caught his hand and pushed back. "You see, I'm not a weakling like she was. You can't treat me that way."

Across the yard, Dora lowered her spyglass, and thought, *Good for you.*

"Mama! Mama! Come see my dress," called Lottie.

"On my way, baby."

CHAPTER 29

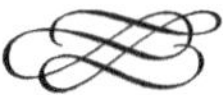

The musicians had arrived, and they were setting up in the foyer. Clair had provided a three-string quartet for the party.

There was a knock on the door, and Dora opened it. She saw Thomas, Clair, and their daughter Mary Elizabeth standing there. "Merry Christmas!" the trio said.

"Merry Christmas to you!" she replied. "Come in out of the cold." Once they were inside, she took their coats and knelt next to Mary Elizabeth. "Are you excited for Christmas?"

"Yes! Where's your tree?" she asked, looking around.

"We have two. One over there," Dora pointed to one near the musicians, "and one in the sitting room." Mary Elizabeth ran toward the sitting room.

Clair laughed. "She's been checking all the presents at home for her name."

"She'll find some under ours. It's good to see you." Dora leaned over and kissed Clair and Thomas on the cheek.

"The place looks festive," Thomas observed.

"Yes, Christmas should be festive."

"I agree."

Lottie and Hen came in from the dining room. They went over to greet the couple. "Is Mary Elizabeth here?" Lottie asked Clair.

"In the sitting room," she told the little girl.

Hen and Lottie ran into the sitting room to greet her. Dora followed them and said, "You two aren't even dressed yet."

"We're going up now." Hen took Lottie's hand and walked her to the stairs.

Dora looked down at her dress. "I think I need to head up also." She turned to Clair and Thomas. "You sit and let Ethyl know if you need anything."

"We will," Thomas assured her.

Dora walked quickly and started up the stairs. Emma was descending in a burgundy velvet dress, her hair up in a red ribbon. "Our guests will be arriving soon," she reminded her sister.

"I'm on my way to change," Dora told her. "Clair, Thomas and Mary Elizabeth are here."

"I'll keep them company." Emma continued downstairs and into the sitting room. She walked over to Clair. "You look lovely." Her friend was wearing a dark blue dress with velvet trim.

"So do you," Clair responded.

"Where's Mary Elizabeth?"

"Over at the tree with Thomas. They're searching for gifts."

Emma laughed. "Dora and I used to do the same. You're a little early."

"I thought we might want to compare notes before the party starts."

"And before the villains arrive." Emma grinned. "Come sit down." They sat on the settee while Thomas tried to get the gifts back under the tree.

Mary Elizabeth ran over to her; her dress was identical to her mother's. "Hi, Emma!"

"Merry Christmas," Emma replied, leaning over to kiss her head. "Would you like something sweet?"

She grinned. "Yes, please."

"Thomas, Ethyl's finishing with the setup. Why don't you check with her?"

"I'll do that." He looked down at his daughter. "Will you share something with me?" he asked her.

"Maybe."

He laughed. "We'll be in the kitchen." He and Mary Elizabeth started toward the kitchen to see what sweets they could coax out of Ethyl. The musicians began playing, and the music floated into the room.

"We appreciate your help," Emma told her friend.

"I don't mind at all. The man's slime. Some of my girls had people like him in their lives. It ruined them."

Emma took her hand. "We'll get him."

"You want me to turn on my charm again?" Clair asked.

"Yes. We need time over at the house."

Clair grinned wolfishly. "I'll do that, and I'll get more money out of him."

CHAPTER 30

*D*ora finished fixing Lottie's hair. Emma had had enough lace left over and she added it to Lotties green dress. "Would you like a bow in your hair?"

"Yes, please."

Dora clipped it in Lottie's hair and stepped back. Her auburn hair was curled and flowed down her back. "You look beautiful."

"Mama, you need to get dressed," Lottie reminded her.

She glanced at her watch. "Why don't you go join Papa downstairs?"

"Okay, Mama." Lottie stopped at the door. "Are you feeling better?"

"I am. I'll get dressed now, I promise." Dora watched her daughter leave and walked to the side table to get out the spyglass. She moved to the side window and pushed the curtains back just enough to get the glass through, checking from window to window. She saw a movement upstairs and thought, *Those people really need to invest in curtains.*

Mrs. Smythe was in the bedroom and seemed to be looking for something. Dora watched her drag a chair to the closet. She seemed to be reaching inside and came back with nothing. "Not there," murmured Dora. Mrs. Smythe moved out of her sight and then appeared again as she hastened across the room. She held up her hand. "What'd she find?" Dora asked, squinting through the glass. Smythe entered the room, and the woman immediately put her hand behind her back.

"Looking for something?" Tim asked from the doorway.

Dora jumped. "Ah! You scared me!"

"See anything?" he asked, glancing out the window.

"No."

She handed the spyglass to him. He held it up to his eyes and looked out the window. "I don't see anything."

"I was watching Mrs. Smythe."

"Was she doing anything interesting?"

"It looked like she was searching for something."

"Did she find it?"

"I think so. She was holding something in her hand, and I don't think she wants him to know what she found. As soon as he came into the room, she hid it."

"Hmm… more to watch tonight."

She noticed he had on his suit for the party. "Oh, I'm so late."

"You are. I came up to tell you people are starting to arrive."

"I'll hurry. You can go downstairs."

He checked his watch. "I'll head down now." He waved and left the room, closing the door behind him.

Dora pulled out her dress and laid it on the bed. She'd put her hair up earlier. She walked to the mirror and checked it, patting a few stray hairs and adding her makeup. There was a quick knock on her door. Emma stuck her head in the crack.

"Need some help?"

"Please. I sent Tim away before I realized I couldn't do up the back of my dress."

"I'm here now." She helped Dora get it on. "Turn and we'll take care of it." She turned, and Emma did up the buttons. "All done," she said and patted her on the back.

Dora grabbed her lace shawl, and they walked out together. "Are they here yet?" There was only one couple they were concerned about that night.

"Not yet."

"What if they don't show up?"

"We'll think of another way in," Emma said firmly. Dora frowned. "What is it?"

"Jimmy. I don't want him to have to stay in that job. Especially if we don't stop Dr. Smythe tonight."

"Tim and I talked about him. We can easily add him to our temp agency. I understand he's a good handyman."

"Hen said he's very intelligent," Dora suggested.

"I've been thinking about that." The music wafted up the stairs. "Come on, time to join the party."

They walked down the stairs; Tim and Jeremy met them at the bottom. Emma and Jeremy walked to the dining room, while Tim took Dora's hand and said, "You're the prettiest girl here."

"Thank you." She blushed. "It's a full house," she said, looking around.

"So far, they aren't here," he said in a low voice. He knew who she was looking for.

"Where's Jimmy?"

"He's here. Don't worry, Hen's keeping an eye on him."

"Good."

They started through the crowd. Greetings and Merry Christmas rang throughout the foyer.

Knocking sounded from the door. Tim quickly opened it. Standing there was Dr. Smythe and his wife. Tim started to make a fist. Dora saw it and put her hand on his, covering it up. "Merry Christmas," she told the couple. "Please, come in." Mrs. Smythe entered ahead of her husband. Tim shut the door, and he and Dora moved to help them with their coats.

When Mrs. Smythe uncovered her hair and revealed her face, Dora gasped.

"Is something wrong?" Smythe asked, watching her closely.

Tim grasped her hand. "She's just feeling a little dizzy still, that's all."

"That's right, could you find me a chair?" she asked Tim.

"Of course. Enjoy yourselves." Tim walked her quickly to the kitchen. As she sat down, he looked at her. "Are you okay?"

"Get me some water, please." The temporary maids were in the kitchen, and she didn't feel free to talk.

"Can you take some trays out to the guest?" Tim told them. They nodded and picked up the trays to circulate in the other rooms. He walked to the sink.

"Not water," Dora said. "The rum punch."

He raised his eyebrows. "You're sure?"

"I am," she said firmly.

He got her a cup, and she drank it all down at once. "What'd you see?"

"I knew that Jimmy said she looked just like the other woman. It was just shocking to see a dead woman in our foyer." She took a deep breath. "Shouldn't we get back out there?"

"Everyone's watching them; we can take a moment."

She stood and took a couple of deep breaths. "Okay, I'm ready."

He offered her his arm, and they went into the dining room. Ellis and Abbey stood by the fireplace. "Go on and circulate," she told him. "I want to talk to Abbey." He nodded and watched her go over to the fireplace. "Abbey, can I speak with you?"

"Of course." Abbey moved close to her. "What's going on?"

"Can you take a look at the ring on Mrs. Smythe's hand?" They'd explained the case and what would happen at the party when they arrived earlier.

"I can. What're you thinking?"

"I think she's wearing the dead wife's ring."

Abbey frowned at this. "How can I help with that?"

"Can you ask her to see it? Make sure he's there when you ask."

"Why?"

"Because I don't think he wants her to be wearing it."

Abbey nodded, walked over to Ellis, and whispered in his ear. He nodded and accompanied her into the foyer.

Dora moved to the doorway to watch. Ellis and Abbey mingled with different groups and slowly made their way to the doctor and his wife. They spoke for a few moments, and she shot a look at her husband before she flashed the ring.

Smythe's response was immediate; he grabbed her arm and pulled. She didn't budge. He finally smiled and said something to her. The two moved toward the hallway. Emma had been watching and motioned to Tim that she'd follow the couple.

Smythe walked his wife to the basement door, opened it, and forced her inside. Emma stood at the door, listening.

"Why do you have that ring?" Smythe demanded.

"You mean this?" she asked. "It's mine, after all. I *am* your wife."

"I told you that ring was off limits."

"Yeah, well, I don't like all these rules, and maybe I'll want to be moving on next."

"Maybe you'll move on tonight," he growled.

She laughed loudly. "Ha, no. I'll move on when I want to, and I'll be taking all of the fine jewels with me."

"Those are mine!" he roared back.

She laughed again, and their voices cut off suddenly. Emma decided it was time to interrupt. She called out loudly, "Jeremy, I'm going down to get that bottle from the basement." She opened the door, and the couple broke apart. "Oh, I'm sorry, did you get lost?" she asked, concerned.

"Oh, I guess we did," Mrs. Smythe said, holding a hand to her neck as she moved quickly past Emma.

Smythe moved more slowly and stopped beside Emma. "If you don't want people down here, I'd keep the room locked."

It's a basement, jackass. People usually don't wander into strangers' basements, she thought to herself. Instead, she smiled sweetly and said, "Oh gosh, I didn't think of that. I'll make sure to do that in the future." As they walked away, she noticed the red marks on Mrs. Smythe's neck. *Gotta end this before he kills another wife. Sure hope he doesn't have even more duplicates.*

She walked back out to the party. Mrs. Smythe had abandoned her husband and had started to circulate. A maid walked by, and she grabbed a glass of champagne and drank it down in one gulp. She grabbed another glass before the maid could leave and drank it down, too.

Emma moved to where Jeremy stood with Cole. "The fun should be starting now." She filled them in on what'd happened in the basement. Smythe stood by himself, staring across the room. "He's watching Dora. We need a distraction." Emma nodded to Clair.

She acknowledged her with a nod and walked smoothly over to the doctor. His face brightened, and she spoke animatedly to him.

"She does seem to hypnotize the man," Cole observed.

"That's why she's a good director for the charity. They just hand over checks to her."

"What now?" Jeremy asked.

.

CHAPTER 31

Clair looked at Smythe. "Excuse me, I need to check on something. I'll have to leave you for a little while."

"Of course." Smythe stared after her. A man bumped his shoulder hard. He looked and saw a red-headed man with scars on his face.

"Sorry about that," Thomas said. He shoved Smythe hard against the wall. "Sorry, the place is crowded."

Smythe frowned and started to push him back. Clair called, "Thomas!" Thomas waved to her.

"You know Ms. Callahan?" Smythe asked.

"She's *my* wife," Thomas stressed. "Maybe you should find yours." He released the doctor and walked over to stand with Clair.

Smythe looked around and found Dora. She was moving through the foyer into the dining room. He followed her, passing a few maids.

Dora went into the kitchen to retrieve another tray of cookies. She heard the door swing open, and she said, "I could use a hand here." When no response came, she turned around.

Smythe stood so close to her that his suit jacket brushed her dress. Her eyes went wide.

"I wanted to respond to your letter in person," he growled.

"Wha...? What letter?" she stammered. "I don't know what you're talking about." Dora tried to back up but the counter bore into her back.

"The letter that you put in my house," Smythe spat. "You had your sister come to take it back, but I read it." He moved closer, holding up his hands.

"You won't get away with it! We have a lot more guests here tonight who can be witnesses. You'll be caught."

"Yes, but you'll be gone."

"Why'd you kill your wife?" she blurted.

"I didn't kill my wife." He grinned wolfishly. "You can see her at the party."

"I see someone who looks like her," she acknowledged.

"If I had killed my wife—and I didn't, since she's at this party —she might have had the same issue you do, sticking your nose into places it doesn't belong. You need to stay out of my business."

"You mean your drug business?" Dora asked.

"What do you know about that?" Smythe asked with narrowed eyes.

"I know that first you tried to kill me with a pillow, and when that didn't work, you gave me the bottle of opium."

"Your husband and sister came back too soon. There are too many people around here. I kept getting interrupted. But not anymore."

"You do choose bad locations," Dora said. Smythe wrapped his hands around her neck. Before he could squeeze, she called out, "Got that?"

"Got what?" he growled as he started to tighten his hands around her neck.

Cole stepped out of the pantry holding a gun on Smythe.

"Let her go." When he didn't lower his hands, Cole cocked his gun.

Smythe finally loosened his hands and dropped them to his sides. Dora wheezed and pushed him away from her.

Tim, Jeremy, Ellis, and Abbey rushed into the kitchen. Emma followed, dragging Mrs. Smythe with her. "I think it's time you took us on a tour of your basement," Cole said.

"You bitch!" Smythe screamed and lunged at Dora.

Tim grabbed him by the collar and yanked him back. "You wanna try that on me, boyo?"

Smythe swung his fist. Tim moved his head back and punched him in the face. As Smythe went down, Tim lifted his leg and kneed the man in the face. Smythe fell to the floor, and Tim bent to pick him up.

Emma, afraid Tim was going to kill the man, stepped forward. "Tim, we need him alive to show us where the body's located."

Tim looked at her and nodded. He pulled Smythe upright and shook him. Smythe moaned and opened his eyes. "Smythe, can you hear me? The only reason you're not seeing the devil right now is we need you to show us where you hid the body."

Mrs. Smythe smirked. "They gotcha, Robbie. He isn't a doctor," she told everyone. "It's all fake."

"She... She's part of this!" Smythe yelled.

They looked at her. "I can show you the basement," she said.

He screamed again. Cole waved to his men standing outside. They came in and took custody of the doctor. "Jones, tie him up and keep him here."

Smythe dropped to the floor, trying to get away from them. They jumped on him and had him secure in a few seconds.

"You know, Robbie, you shouldn't take your own product. Makes you crazy." Mrs. Smythe smirked,

Cole waved the gun at her. "All right, time to take that tour."

She sighed and nodded. "I haven't been down there, but I know where the keys are."

They opened the kitchen door to go to the doctor's house. They didn't want to drag the prisoners through the party. Hen rushed into the kitchen with their coats and hats, with Jimmy accompanying her.

"I want to go," he said.

Emma looked at him and shook her head. "Look, we don't know what we're going to find, and it might not be pretty. Please stay here. We'll tell you what's down there once it's over." He clenched his hands, but stayed where he was.

"Hen," Dora said softly, "please."

She nodded and took Jimmy's hand. "Here, I'll wait with you."

He said, "I'll be here." The group walked out together. "Wait!" he called from the door. They stopped and looked at him. He looked at Mrs. Smythe. "I know you're not Susan. Who are you?"

"You knew along I wasn't her, didn't you?" He nodded. She looked at Smythe, who glared at her. "I'm Mandy. Susan was my twin."

"Let's go," Emma said. "We can get more information after."

They exited and walked through the snow to the doctor's house. Mandy opened the door; they all went into the foyer and to the basement door. "Is this a new door?" Jeremy asked.

"Yeah, we had a break-in the night of the gala." She looked at them, and something clicked. "Ohh, that was you, wasn't it?"

Emma looked at Dora. "You and Tim need to stay up here."

"No," Dora said firmly. "I want to be there."

"Me too," Tim said.

Emma nodded and looked at Mandy. "Key?"

"Yeah, it's in the kitchen." Cole accompanied her, and they returned with the keys. "Follow me." As they walked down the stairs, they turned up the gas lamps. At the bottom, they saw long corridors branching off. She went down the first one to a metal door.

Emma walked over and ran her hand down it. "Got a key for this lock?"

"I only knew the room existed; I don't have access to that lock. Robbie probably has it with him."

"I don't need him," Emma told her. She pulled a lockpick kit out of her pocket and knelt next to the door. It took a few minutes; the lock was large, and the tumblers were harder to maneuver. It finally clicked, and she moved back. Jeremy took the handle and pulled it open forcefully.

The smell hit them first. Mandy scrunched up her nose and retched. "I can take her back up," Cole volunteered.

"No," Dora said, "she's part of this; she should be a witness to whatever we find." Mandy nodded. Dora waited for Emma to light her torch. "Was that a growl?" she asked. A low growl came again. They all went quiet. "Could Tams still be alive?" she asked.

They didn't guess. Emma went in first with her torch, Jeremy close behind.

"She's here!" Emma called.

"So's Tams," Jeremy said.

Dora wiped her eyes and gripped Tim's hand.

"Tim, I think we're going to need you," Jeremy said.

Tim let go of Dora's hand and entered the dark room. Dora squinted, trying to see what they were doing.

"Step back, we're coming out," Emma said. Dora, Cole, and Mandy moved back against the wall. Tim came out first, carrying Susan.

"Is she alive?" Mandy asked.

"She is, for now," Tim said. "We need to get her out of here."

Cole and Mandy followed them up and out. Dora started to follow him when Jeremy appeared with Tams. The dog was skin and bones. He used his little bit of energy to lick Jeremy's hand. Emma came out of the room with a frown on her face.

"They're alive," Dora said, relieved.

"They're out. I hope they're able to survive. We need Jake down here to take pictures. I want the court to see what Smythe did and hold him responsible for it."

"He's at the party," Dora confirmed. "We'll get him to come over when we call the police."

CHAPTER 32

"How did he set all this up?" Cole asked Mandy. The party had broken up, and only the family remained at the house. They were seated in the dining room, listening to her confession.

"Robbie married Susan in Maine; she thought he was a real doctor. He told her they'd start a practice and a family. She believed him; she was so naïve," she scoffed.

"She didn't trust him," Jimmy told her. Cole had Jimmy in the room to fill in the details.

"How do you know that?" she asked.

"She was trying to leave him. She'd seen too many families broken apart by the opium. I'd bought her a train ticket back home the day she disappeared."

"Robbie thought she might be planning something like that. He contacted me and told me there was money for me if I came here and took her place."

"Even though he killed your sister?" Dora asked her.

"Hey, I am not a nice person. I admit that." She looked at Jimmy. "How'd you know I wasn't her?"

"It was Tams. She didn't like you."

"That damn dog," Mandy griped.

"Can I go see Tams?" Jimmy asked Cole.

"I don't see a problem with that." He nodded at Tim. Tim took Jimmy and left the room.

Jeremy walked in. "The police are here to take him downtown."

"I think we have what we need for now." Cole looked at Mandy. "By the way, you're under arrest."

She nodded glumly. "Yeah, I kinda thought so." She stood and put her hands behind her back.

Cole stepped out of the house with Smythe and Mandy in handcuffs. The police were waiting for them outside. Crowds had formed around them when a shot sounded out, and everyone looked around wildly. Smythe fell forward, dead. Jones and another agent pulled a man forward; he had a knife in his arm.

Emma stepped from behind them. "I'm going to need that knife back when you're done with it," she told Jones.

Cole bent down and turned Smythe over. The bullet had gone through his head.

"I'm glad he's dead!" the man yelled as the Pinkerton agents hauled him off. "He killed my son! He got what he deserved!"

That night, after everyone was home and in bed, Jeremy turned to Emma. "Babe, I have to ask. Did you see the gun?"

"Are you asking if I waited to throw my knife until after Smythe was shot?" she asked.

He nodded.

"The punishment seemed to fit the crime. Susan and Tams barely made it through alive. And that poor man, losing his son to that drug." She lifted her head off his chest. "I'm concerned that there'll be more people showing up wanting their medication."

"We'll need to discuss with the group how to handle the situation."

"Tomorrow," she said and laid her head back down.

He pulled her close, and they went to sleep.

CHAPTER 33

Tim, Jeremy, Emma, and Dora sat in the dining room reviewing what'd happened the night before. "How are Susan and Tams?" Dora asked.

"Susan's at the hospital and stable," Jeremy said. "They're having to give her food slowly, as too much at this stage could still kill her."

"We need to stop by and see her," Dora said.

"We'll take her some things today," Tim promised. "I've been thinking about Smythe's house. I talked to Dr. Phillips and asked him to come over and talk about options." They heard someone knocking on the door. Tim checked his watch. "That should be him now." He stood and hurried to the door.

Emma and Jeremy looked at Dora. She shrugged. "This is all Tim."

"Thanks for coming on Christmas Eve," Tim said, escorting Dr. Phillips into the dining room.

"Tim explained to me what was happening next door. He was concerned after the father of one of the patients showed up here last night. I wanted to come see how I can help," Dr. Phillips said.

"I found out that the house was leased and not owned by Smythe," Tim told the group. "I've always planned to buy it, and so this morning I made an offer for it."

"Did they accept it?" Dora asked him.

"They did. Eventually, we can use it for another boarding house. For now, we'll house the more severe opium cases, and hopefully have Dr. Phillips here, or someone he can recommend, to monitor their withdrawal."

"How can we stop this from happening?" Emma asked.

"Educating doctors is the key," Dr. Phillips stressed. "That man, Smythe, was not a doctor, but even real doctors give out opium too easily."

"We may not have enough time. What if people come before the house is set up?" Dora asked.

"We'll hospitalize them until it's finished," Tim replied.

CHAPTER 34

Christmas morning, Patrick, Lottie, and Hen were running about the house, knocking on doors, calling, "Get up, it's Christmas!"

"I'm coming," Emma called back. "Up, sleepy head." She nudged him. "Jeremy, Christmas is here."

"I know what I want for Christmas," he said and pulled her to him. She sank into him and then heard another knock at the door. "Getting up now." They broke apart, and he headed to his room. The bookcase door closed, and she pulled on her robe to open the door. Hen sat outside.

"Ready?" she asked excitedly.

"Bathroom first," Emma said.

Hen pouted and sat back down and waited. Emma hurried, and when she finished, she walked back down the hall. "Merry Christmas!" she said and hugged Hen.

Hen hugged back. "Thanks for inviting Jimmy," she said as they walked back into Emma's room.

"He needs us," Emma said, pulling out her dress and laying it on the bed.

"Like me."

Emma walked over and kissed Henrietta on the head. "Yes. We have some plans for him."

"What are they?"

"Well, school for one," Emma told her firmly.

"Ohh, I'm not sure he's going to like that. He wants to be able to support himself."

"We're working on that also." Emma pulled on her red dress and put on a black belt. She sat and pulled on her boots. Fully dressed, she held out her hand. "Let's get Jeremy and go downstairs."

"Finally!"

They went out the door and found Jeremy waiting. "Merry Christmas, Henreitta."

"Merry Christmas, Jeremy."

"Merry Christmas, Emma."

"You too," she said with a grin.

Dora called up from the foyer, "Are you guys finally up?"

"We are," Emma called back.

"Well, come down already! We're burning daylight!"

When they got downstairs, they heard knocking at the door. Patrick ran to the door and found Jimmy there, and he was carrying Tams.

"How is she?" Patrick asked him.

"She's doing better, but I don't want to leave her alone. Is it okay if I bring her in?"

Patrick yelled out, "Papa, can Tams come in for Christmas?"

"Of course. We have a place set up for her in the sitting room."

Jimmy let out the breath he was holding. He grinned and walked into the house. "Merry Christmas."

"You too." Patrick asked, "Can I pet her?"

"Yes, lightly, though." Patrick reached over to pet the dog. She licked his hand, and Patrick grinned.

Tim walked up and said, "Let me take your coat." Jimmy frowned; he didn't want to set Tams down.

"I'll hold her," Patrick volunteered. Jimmy looked torn. "I'll be careful," he promised.

Jimmy nodded and handed the dog to him. He took off his coat and saw that Tams was licking Patrick's neck, making him laugh.

Dora looked around. "Who're we still waiting for?"

"Ellis, Abbey, Cole, and Amy," said Tim.

Emma frowned. "Are John and Jemma already here?"

"I got here earlier," John called from the dining room entrance. He was carrying a small girl. Jeremy grinned and went over to get her. She saw him and held out her arms; John shifted Jemma over to him.

"Are Catherine and Sam going to join us?" Emma asked him. They were Jemma's parents.

"No, they're traveling and we'll have an addition next Christmas."

"Another grandchild, John?" asked Dora.

"Yes, they told me before they left."

"Congratulations!" came from around the foyer.

"Thank you," he said with a nod of his head.

Lottie ran over and grabbed Jeremy's legs. "Hold me, Uncle Jeremy," she said.

Emma walked over and picked her up. "How about me instead?"

"Okay," she said, frowning at Jemma.

"What's the matter, Lottie?" Emma asked her.

"Why does Jeremy want to hold her and not me?"

Whoa, Emma thought, *she really does not like Jemma.* She tried to distract her. "What are you looking forward to for Christmas?" Lottie didn't say anything but continued to stare at Jemma. "Presents? Desserts? Candy?"

That distracted her. "All of them," Lottie said. "Down please." Emma set her down and she ran into the dining room.

Cool air blasted from the door. More family had arrived! Amy, Cole, Ellis, and Abbey. "Merry Christmas!" rang out.

The last group had arrived at the door; Thomas, Clair, and Mary Elizabeth had arrived.

Greeting were made, coats were taken, and Dora said, "Breakfast."

Everyone went to the loaded table. Ethyl and Jake were already seated. The group joined them, blessings were said, and Christmas Day started.

HISTORICAL NOTES

Addiction is not a new thing; my story is set in 1891 and involves a significant amount of opiates being given out by doctors. The opium problem did not change until there was significant doctor education on the addictive properties of the drug. Opiates continue to be a problem in the 21st century, where it is entirely too easy to service outside of a doctor's care.

Slang-Like every era, teenagers use slang to express themselves. I n 1891, Chicago, the colorful language reflected the terms they lived in. See below for definitions of slang used in this book:

Shinning around - Moving about.

Arf'arf'an'arf - A figure of speech used to describe drunken men.

Lally-cooler - A real success.

Chuckaboo - A nickname given to a close friend.

Jammiest bits of jam - An absolutely perfect young female.

Wake snakes — Get into mischief.

Too high for his nut — Beyond someone's reach.

Not up to Dick - Not well.

Basket of Oranges - Refers to a pretty woman.

Damfino - A contraction of "damned if I know."

Mutton Shunter - Term for a policeman. So much better than "pig."

Some pumpkins - A big deal

Dizzy Age - Meaning elderly.

Mad as Hops - Used to describe something exciting.

To be Chicagoed — To be beaten soundly.

Enthuzimuzzy - A satirical reference to enthusiasm.

Orf chump - No appetite.

Batty-fang - To thrash thoroughly.

Notebook Mysteries

KIMBERLY MULLINS

ABOUT THE AUTHOR

Kimberly Mullins is the author of series of books titled "Notebook Mysteries". Her stories are based on historical events occurring in 1871-1890's Chicago. She holds a BS in Biology and a MBA in Business. She lives in Texas with her husband and son. When she is not writing she is working as a Process Safety Engineer at a large chemical company. You can connect with her on her website www.kimberlymullinsauthor.com.

Photo Credit: Blessings of Faith Photography

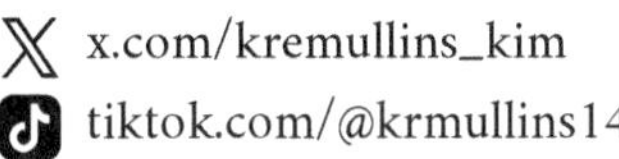

x.com/kremullins_kim

tiktok.com/@krmullins14